A TREASURY OF
STORIES FROM
THE OLD
TESTAMENT

KINGFISHER
Larousse Kingfisher Chambers Inc.
95 Madison Avenue
New York, New York 10016

First American edition 1995
2 4 6 8 10 9 7 5 3 1

LIBRARY OF CONGRESS CATALOGING-IN-PUBLICATION DATA
Pearson, Maggie.
A treasury of Old Testament stories/Maggie Pearson, Kate Aldous.
p. cm.
Summary: A collection of well-known Old Testament stories,
including those about
Adam and Eve, Noah, and David and Goliath.
1. Bible stories, English—O.T. [1. Bible stories—O.T.]
I. Aldous, Kate. II. Title.
BS 551.2.P44 1995   95-1351
221.9'505—dc20
CIP AC

ISBN 1-85697-594-0
Printed in Portugal

A TREASURY OF STORIES FROM
THE OLD TESTAMENT

Retold by
MAGGIE PEARSON

Illustrated by
KATE ALDOUS

Kingfisher

NEW YORK

CONTENTS

7   In the Beginning

12   The Glory of the Garden

21   Mrs. Noah's Story

30   The Perfect Sacrifice

37   Bean Stew

48   The Dreamer of Dreams

54   Joseph in Egypt

66   The Baby in the Basket

75   Let My People Go!

91   One Man and His Donkey

102   Out of the Strong, Something Sweet

119   The Good Daughter

129   Giant-killer!

142   Solomon the Wise

147   Daniel and the Lions

153   The Reluctant Prophet

IN THE BEGINNING

In the beginning, there was only God. God everywhere.

God nowhere. There was no "where" to be.

No heaven, no Earth. No land, no sea. No up, no down. No near, no far.

Just God, dreaming of all the worlds that might be.

How long did God dream? There is no way of saying. There was no time.

God said: "Let there be light!"

And there was light.

For one tiny moment, there was nothing but light, brilliant and blinding, until God separated the light from the darkness.

Then God lifted up the sky as high as it would go and the first day dawned, light dancing on the waves of the eternal sea.

Beautiful, thought God, reaching down through the waters to draw up the land and spreading it out to dry.

As it dried, the land formed itself into hills and valleys, high rocky cliffs, and beaches where the waters lapped against the sand and pebbles.

Perfect. God left the beaches just as they were and moved inland.

Wherever God passed, grass covered the Earth like a carpet, flowers opened in surprise and turned their faces toward the sky. Tall trees sprang up, all in a moment, and spread their branches.

Next, God gathered up the light into a ball to make the sun to shine by day, and the scraps that were left over became the moon and stars, so that the night would never be too dark.

Startled birds appeared in the sky, out of nowhere into here. They fluttered down to perch in the trees (a bit unsteadily at first) and burst into song to celebrate this brave new world.

Out of the waters, the first dolphins leaped and dived, scattering sudden shoals of rainbow-colored fish.

All over the hills and valleys and in the deep,

shady woods, animals stretched and yawned, as if waking out of a long sleep, and found themselves in a world they'd never seen before. They tried out a few steps on unsteady legs. Ran. Jumped. Lay down and wriggled on the soft, sweet grass. Plunged into the waters, splashed around, climbed out again, and shook themselves. Or else stood quietly, eyes closed, letting the soft breeze stroke them.

Everywhere there was life and movement, as if the world were dancing.

And yet . . .

And yet, it still needed something more.

Thoughtfully, God took a small piece of earth and mixed it with a little of the water to make clay.

What shape would I choose to be, God wondered, if I could be one creature in this world I've made?

Carefully God worked the clay. Yes: very good.

What? Only one? Two would be better: they'd be company for one another.

So, out of one, God made two.

A man and a woman.

Adam and Eve.

Gently God breathed life into these creatures of clay and watched over them until they woke.

The world was complete.

THE GLORY OF THE GARDEN

Far to the east, toward the sunrise, God made a garden called Eden for Adam and Eve to live in.

There flowers and fruit clustered together on every tree, and the ground was soft enough to sleep on.

When the wind blew, it was only to fan them cool in the heat of the day. The rain fell soft and warm, to wash away the dust.

"Just one thing you must remember," said God. "You can eat the fruit of any tree, except the tree that is in the middle of the garden. That is the Tree of Knowledge of Good and Evil. If you eat the fruit of that tree, you must die."

That seemed easy enough to remember, with the whole of the rest of the garden to play in.

Imagine the wonder of those first days! The

magic of watching a spider spin its web for the very first time! Discovering the scent of roses, tumbling in a bed of them—for the roses in the garden had no thorns. Imagine hearing the first blackbird's song.

"Listen to the blackbird!" cried Eve.

"Blackbird?" said Adam. "That's not much of a name for it. Anyone can see it's a black bird."

"That's why I called it blackbird," said Eve.

"What about that one, then?"

"Rrrr-ow!" said the bird.

"We'll call that one crow," said Eve.

After that, there seemed to be no end to the names they could invent.

"Lion!" said Adam, opening his mouth wide, like the lion's roar.

"La-a-a-a-amb!" cried Eve. "Butterfly!"

"Don't you mean flutter-by?"

"No, I don't. I mean butterfly."

When they ran out of things to give names to, they started making up words, to see what God would invent to fit them.

Words like: elephant!

There it was, with the "l" of its trunk swinging in front and the "phant" bit lumbering along behind.

"Hippopotamus!"

From out of the mud at the water's edge, the

hippopotamus emerged, still wriggling into its skin.

God laughed. God was pleased. Already these two little creatures were beginning to think for themselves.

At last God grew tired of the game and went away to rest. Adam lay down and went to sleep.

Eve was still too excited. She wandered about, looking for new wonders.

"Nothing to do?" said a voice.

Eve looked up and saw a strange creature hanging from the branch of the Tree of the Knowledge of Good and Evil.

"Oh!" she cried. "What are you?"

The creature smiled: "I am a s-s-s-s-snake," it said. "Do you think the name suits me?"

"I think," said Eve, "that you are the most beautiful creature of all."

"I am, aren't I?" sighed the snake. Lazily it swung, watching Eve with unblinking eyes.

"Are you hungry?" it asked. "Be my guest."

It curled itself around the branch and lay with its chin resting on a cushion of leaves.

Now that he mentioned it, Eve was a bit hungry. She reached out a hand to pick a fruit from the tree. Then she stopped. She remembered what God had said: "You can eat the fruit from any tree, except the tree that is in the middle of the garden."

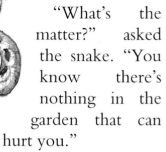

"What's the matter?" asked the snake. "You know there's nothing in the garden that can hurt you."

Eve was puzzled. "What is 'hurt'?" she asked.

"That's for me to know and you to find out," replied the snake.

"I only know," said Eve, frowning, "that if we eat the fruit of this tree, we shall die."

"What is 'die'?" inquired the snake.

"I don't know," said Eve in a very small voice.

"Then how do you know it's not a good thing?"

"Do *you* know?"

"Oh, yes. *I* know."

"Tell me."

"Knowing something you've been told is not the same as knowing something you've found out for yourself. Come on, eat up. You're not afraid, are you?"

"What is 'afraid'?"

16

"You don't know much, do you?" sighed the snake. "Taste the fruit and you'll know all these things. And more. Everything God knows, you'll know. You will be like God."

"I'll just try a little bit." Eve picked one of the fruits and tasted it.

When Adam found her, Eve was sitting crying under the tree. That was something he'd never seen before. Water coming from her eyes! How did she do it?

"Taste the fruit," sniffed Eve, "Then you'll understand."

Without thinking twice, Adam took the fruit and tasted it. At the very first bite, his head was flooded with so many strange thoughts that he forgot to swallow and almost choked. Thoughts of fear and pain and death—and so much more.

He stared at Eve in horror. And Eve stared back.

They saw themselves for what they were— poor, helpless creatures made of clay, without even a covering of fur or feathers.

They did their best to put it right. Nearby was a fig tree. They picked some of the leaves and began trying to figure out a way of fixing them together, by braiding or weaving, into something to wear.

There was another good reason for covering

themselves with leaves.
They knew they'd done
wrong. Perhaps if they
covered themselves with
leaves and crouched
down very small, God
would not find them.

God often passed
through the garden in the
cool of the evening. They
felt the soft whisper of the
breeze through the leaves
that told them God was
near, smelled the scent of
flowers where God
moved.

But already God knew
what they had done. And if they had been able
to make themselves invisible, God would still
have found them. They stood there trembling
in their little aprons of leaves.

"It was Eve's idea, not mine," said Adam.

That was a cowardly thing to do, to blame it
all on Eve, but Adam was afraid and he had
never known fear before.

"It wasn't me," said Eve. "It was the snake."

They all looked around for the culprit, but
the snake had crawled away the moment he
saw trouble brewing, leaving only his empty

skin behind.

God said sadly, "It is time for you to leave the garden."

"No!"

"Please, no!"

"Just give us one more chance!"

"Too late," said God. "You must go out into the world now and make your own way as best you can."

The garden was gone. Where they stood, they could see thistles springing up among the flowers and brambles where the roses grew. The ground felt rough underfoot and a chill wind nipped at their bare skin.

"Don't leave us alone!" begged Adam.

But there was no answer.

Eve took Adam's hand. "We're not alone," she said. "We still have each other."

"We shall die," said Adam.

"Our children will live. And their children. And their children's children. Think of it! People like us, all over the world."

"I'm cold," said Adam.

"So am I."

Poor little creatures! Trying to keep themselves warm with a covering of leaves.

During the night, while they slept, God made the skins of some of the precious animals into clothes for Adam and Eve to wear.

"Clothes out of skins!" remarked Adam, as he put them on. "I could do that!"

Eve was watching the calves with their mothers. Soon she'd worked out how to milk a cow.

Well done! thought God. It will be interesting to see how they get on.

Life was hard, but there were good times too. Times like the harvest and springtime, the birth of their first baby.

God never forgave the snake for what it had done. To this day, the snake has no friends. On its belly it crawls in the dirt, hiding in shadows, afraid of the light, afraid that someone might see it and remember.

Adam and Eve never forgot the glory of the garden.

One day, when they were very, very old, Adam said: "Do you think, perhaps, after we die, God might let us back into the garden?"

"Not that garden," said Eve. "That's gone forever. Perhaps somewhere like it. If we try to be good. We'll have to wait and see, won't we?"

MRS. NOAH'S STORY

"Flood the world!" exclaimed Mrs. Noah. "Why would God want to do that? Just when we're all getting along so nicely!"

"We're not, though," said Noah. "The world's a wicked place."

Mrs. Noah went on quietly spinning for a bit, then, "Flood the world!" she said. "Mountain-tops and all?"

"Don't worry," said Noah. "We're going to be saved. You, me, and the boys—and their wives. I'm going to build an ark."

"An ark! What's that?"

"It's rather a special sort of boat. God's given me the instructions. All I have to do is follow them."

"By the way," said Mrs. Noah. "Where *are* the boys?"

"I—um—sent them on an errand. There are a few things we've got to take with us on the ark."

"That was in the instructions, too, was it?"

"Yes. Well, I suppose I'd better make a start. I've only got a week."

"Silly old man!" said Mrs. Noah softly to herself. She squinted up at the sky. "There can't be that much rain up there! Not to flood the world, mountaintops and all."

She took her spinning and sat outside the door, so she could fend off awkward questions from the neighbors.

"What is it, then?" they wanted to know. "What's Noah up to now?"

"It's an ark," she said.

"Oh. Oh, yes, we can see that now. Of course it's an ark. Er—what's an ark?"

"It's a sort of boat," said Mrs. Noah, busily spinning.

"A boat? But we're miles from the sea!"

Mrs. Noah said nothing. Perhaps she should have done. But they wouldn't have believed her. They would have laughed.

A few days later she had other things to worry about. The boys, Shem, Ham, and Japhet, had started arriving home with the "things" Noah had sent them to fetch.

Things like lions and tigers; pigs and horses; chimpanzees, kangaroos, and hippopotamuses.

Noah had to confess that he hadn't quite told his wife the full story.

"The ark's not just for us. We've got to save the animals, too."

"All of them?" exclaimed Mrs. Noah. "What are you going to feed them on?"

"Feed them on?" said Noah. "Oh, yes! God gave me instructions about that, too . . ."

"I'll see to it," she said. "You go and get on with your ark." Silly old man! She shook her head. All those animals and never a thought about feeding them!

By the seventh day the ark was finished and there wasn't a cloud in the sky.

Mrs. Noah was spinning outside in the sun,

well away from all the noise and fuss of the animals being herded aboard the ark. She wasn't bothered about the first few drops of rain.

"Probably won't be much," she told herself. Then, as the rain began to fall more heavily, "We could do with a drop of rain."

Noah was calling to her to get on board.

Mrs. Noah pretended not to hear, in spite of the rain. She'd been on the point of getting up and going indoors, but that might have given Noah the idea she was taking some notice of him. So she just sat where she was, though she was getting rather wet.

Noah gave up shouting and sent the boys to fetch her.

"You're getting wet," said Shem. "Won't

you come in out of the rain?"

"Pooh!" said Mrs. Noah. She kept spinning. "I'm not bothered by a little bit of rain."

"Don't you want to see the inside of the ark, now that it's finished?" Ham suggested.

"No, thank you," she said, still spinning.

"Just to please us?" begged Japhet.

"You won't get me on that thing," declared Mrs. Noah. "Not unless you carry me!"

So that was what they did, with their mother struggling and protesting all the way: "Put me down, you naughty boys! You wait till I tell your father! Oops! Now I've dropped my spindle. We'll have to go back for it. Put me down, I say! It's only a little rain!"

They carried her onto the ark and into the

cabin and pulled up the gangplank so she couldn't get off again.

To be honest, she was quite glad, because the rain was falling in torrents now. There was thunder and lightning too, right over their heads, and the howling of the wind drowned out all noise from the animals.

"We're moving," said Shem suddenly.

"No, we're not," said Japhet, as the ark settled again.

They had several false starts like that. It took a few days of rain before the flood began.

Then one morning they woke to find themselves drifting slowly down the street, past houses with people clustering on the rooftops. Some of them were trying to put together rafts out of bits of furniture. A few had launched little boats which were filling up with rain faster than their owners could bail. Then there were

no more houses and no more people.

Day after day it rained. Sometimes the sky was so dark that it was hard to tell whether it was day or night. Sometimes they got stuck among the tops of tall trees or up against the side of a mountain, until the waters rose high enough to set them free.

The ark drifted on the waters.

They had no idea where they were or where they were going and not much time to think about it, with all the animals to feed and water, not to mention the mucking out.

Mrs. Noah got it all organized, with a proper roster, so everybody did their bit. She asked the boys to shear the sheep they'd brought, and she made herself a spindle so that she could sit quietly spinning whenever she had a spare moment. It made her feel more normal. It can't rain forever, she told herself sensibly. It's got to stop sometime.

And it did stop.

Noah crossed off the day on the calendar he'd made on the wall. Forty days exactly.

All around the ark was nothing but water. No sign of any of the little boats or homemade rafts. No sign of life at all.

Beneath the ark, of course, the waters were teeming with life. Puzzled fish explored the sunken forests. Dolphins swam lazily up and down the city streets, in and out of houses, palaces and temples, wondered whether to move in and decided against it.

On and on sailed the ark, day after day, month after month, until— bump!—it ran aground.

"The waters must be going down!" said Noah. "Let's find out for sure."

He took one of the ravens and one of the doves and let them go. They never saw the raven again, but by nightfall the dove was back.

"We'll wait a week," said Noah. "Then try again."

Each day Mrs. Noah sat spinning in the sun. She'd finished the sheep's wool long ago and started on the goat's hair.

One day, toward evening, Noah came rushing along the deck, clutching the dove in both hands.

"Careful!" she said, "You'll crush it."

"Look!" cried Noah. "Look what he's

holding in his beak!" It was a tiny sprig of olive leaves.

"The waters must be going down at last," breathed Noah. "He's come back to tell us that we're saved!"

He was right. A few days later they could see where they were.

"Wouldn't you know it!" Mrs. Noah exclaimed. "We're right on top of a mountain."

Day after day they watched as the waters slowly went down. Like the world beginning all over again, she thought, the land rising up out of the waters, little by little; the trees, with streamers of seaweed drying in the wind and fish like silver fruit caught up in the branches; the grass slowly creeping over the land, as if God were walking there. And up in the sky glowed the most beautiful rainbow.

That's where we'll build our house," said Mrs. Noah softly, "at the end of the rainbow."

"It's a sign," said Noah. "A promise from God. The world will never be flooded again."

THE PERFECT SACRIFICE

They were a wandering people. Nomads, herding their flocks of sheep and goats from place to place, wherever the old man led them. From Ur, north to Haran, then westward for a while, then finally turning south into the land of Canaan.

Sometimes they had to cross barren lands, but the old man always managed to find grazing and sweet water. Sometimes they camped for a while in a lush, green valley. Then one day the old man would say, "It is time to go," and they would fold their tents and follow where he led.

The old man's name was Abraham. Abraham always knew which way to go, because God told him.

Who would lead them when Abraham was

gone? No one knew.

His first wife, Sarah, had no children. He had other wives and they had sons and daughters. Good children, all of them, but not one that stood out from the rest. Sarah was still his best-beloved, but she was now too old to have children.

Then one night, he heard God's voice, clear as a bell: "Sarah is going to have a baby."

Next morning, Abraham looked for the signs, as he always did, that what God told him was true.

There was no doubt about it, Sarah did look a little plumper. Her skin was clear, with a sort of glow about it, as if she'd just washed in very cold water. There was a brightness in her eyes, a spring in her step, though even she didn't know the reason yet.

The rest of the tribe couldn't help noticing the change in Abraham.

"What's got into the old man?"

"He's looking ten years younger these days."

"More like twenty!"

Abraham said nothing to anyone. When Sarah announced she was expecting a baby—"I didn't want to say anything, but I've been to the midwife and she's sure!"—he acted as if it came as a complete surprise.

The baby was perfect: ten fingers, ten toes,

big eyes, staring up at him, and a cap of dark, brown hair.

"He's got your nose," smiled Sarah.

"I hope not!" Abraham exclaimed. "I wouldn't wish my nose on any baby!"

"Your ears, then. He's got your ears."

"Perhaps," said Abraham.

They named the baby Isaac. He grew into a tall, strong boy. He would make a fine leader for the tribe. Abraham hoped he would live long enough to teach young Isaac all that he knew.

Then one night as he lay awake in the darkness that comes just before the dawn, Abraham heard God's voice again. And what he heard chilled his blood to the very marrow of his bones.

First thing next morning he was on his feet and calling Isaac to him: "Fetch a load of wood," he said, "and come with me. We have to make a special sacrifice."

The boy was puzzled. It was nowhere near the time for the spring festival, when a lamb would be picked out from the flock to sacrifice to God. But he did as he was told, put on his warm cloak and bundled up some kindling. The rest could be gathered nearer the place— wherever that was.

"Where are we going?" asked Isaac.

Abraham lifted up his head toward the distant hills. "Somewhere up there. I'll know the place when we get there."

Isaac's heart beat faster. A special sacrifice. In a secret place.

Any sacrifice, of course, was special. A job for the head of the family, the chief of the tribe. He was proud to think his father had chosen him to help. He wouldn't let him down. Without a glance to left or right, Abraham strode through the camp with Isaac following along behind.

"Where's the old man off to?"

"Some kind of special sacrifice, I heard."

"Hasn't he forgotten something, then?"

"What?"

"The lamb. The lamb for the sacrifice."

No one stood in his way. No one tried to remind him. There was a look on Abraham's face that stopped them.

"He'll be back."

"He'll be back, as soon as he remembers."

"Or else send the boy."

"He won't thank any of us for pointing out he's getting a bit forgetful."

Old men do forget things. But Abraham hadn't forgotten. He was taking the sacrifice, just as the voice had told him to do. His perfect lamb. Isaac.

Not once had he ever disobeyed God and he had always seen good reasons afterward for what He told him to do. Now he looked in vain for some sign and saw only a perfect summer's day; warm sun over green hills and a cool breeze whispering, "This way. This way!"

So this way they went, but not too fast. Let the boy enjoy this one perfect day. Isaac, carrying the growing load of wood, leaped up and down the rocky paths, nimble as a young goat, chased butterflies and lizards, or waded into cool mountain streams to fetch Abraham a cup of water.

As the way grew steeper, he stopped playing and slowed down to Abraham's pace, helping him over difficult bits. "Not far now, Father Nearly there."

"How do you know?"

"We must be nearly there. We're almost top of the world!"

"Yes. This is the place."

"Sit down then and rest. I'll build the fire for the sacrifice. There's just one thing, Father," said Isaac as he worked. "Where is the animal for the sacrifice?"

No answer.

Isaac turned and found Abraham standing just behind him, with his knife ready in his hand.

"You are the sacrifice."

He whispered so softly that Isaac barely heard.

"You are the sacrifice. God demands it."

Abraham turned away and began sharpening his knife on a stone. His eyes were dazzled, with sunlight and with tears, but he didn't hesitate.

"You gave me my son, Lord. Now take him back, if you must. Only help me to strike true. I can't see for tears."

The light grew brighter and from out of the brightness God's voice came, stronger than he'd ever heard it before, but gentle, too: "Abraham, my faithful servant! Look in the thicket below you."

Abraham opened his eyes and looked.

He saw something white among the bushes.

Slowly the old man picked his way down the slope, with Isaac running ahead of him, to where a snow white ram stood tangled in the thicket.

"Wherever did he come from?" Isaac cried. "There can't be a flock of sheep for miles! Stay here! I'll get him."

"Careful, then, or you'll scratch him." Abraham's voice was trembling. "He must be perfect for the sacrifice."

Patiently the ram stood, while Isaac untangled him from the brambles.

And Abraham heard God's voice again: "Because you have obeyed me without question—because you would have given me your son—your people shall become a great nation."

Together, Abraham and Isaac made the sacrifice.

The smoke rose upward, straight to heaven.

Before they sat down to share the meat, Abraham gave Isaac his blessing. "You will be the next leader of our tribe," he said. "I know it now, without a shadow of a doubt."

Afterward, when they had eaten, the boy led the way down the mountain.

And the old man followed him.

BEAN STEW

You'd never have taken them for brothers, never mind twins. There was Jacob, fine-boned, fair-skinned, but good with the sheep.

And there was Esau. Ever since he learned to throw a spear, he'd spent most of his time off hunting. He dressed in the skins of the animals he killed, and sometimes it was hard to tell where the skins ended and Esau began, with his hairy chest and his long hair and his beard always in need of a trim. He smelled, too.

"That's good, honest sweat, that is!" said Esau cheerfully, whenever it got so bad that Rebecca, their mother, felt she had to mention it.

Rebecca sighed. Esau, my eldest son! she thought. The one who's going to inherit everything. All because he happened to be born first!

It had been a close thing. When the twins were born, Jacob had emerged holding tight to Esau's foot, as if he'd been doing his best to overtake him. Or as if Esau was kicking him out of the way . . .

Rebecca was sure of it. Jacob was always meant to be first. It wasn't her darling boy's fault if that loudmouthed idiot had shoved him aside.

There was never any doubt which one Isaac, their father, preferred. He was growing old, stiff in his joints, and going blind. His great pleasure in life now was to hear Esau telling tales of his latest hunt.

While Jacob and Rebecca sat, not bothering to hide their yawns and giving each other long-suffering looks, the old man, in his mind's eye, would be following his son, the mighty hunter, every step of the way.

It was no good trying to persuade Isaac that Jacob would make a much better heir.

"What does Esau know about keeping sheep?" Rebecca said. "He's never here."

"He is my eldest son," Isaac insisted.

"*You* weren't the eldest," Rebecca pointed out. "I had a dream before they were born and in my dream God told me that the older boy would serve the younger one. God wants Jacob to be your heir."

"If that's what God wants, then God will arrange it," said Isaac.

She might as well have talked to the wind. But Rebecca was not the sort of woman who gives up easily.

"You shall have your birthright," she promised Jacob.

Say what you like about Rebecca, but she was a very good cook. With nothing but a handful of beans, a few vegetables, and herbs, she could make a dish fit for a king. It was just as well, because sometimes Esau was away hunting for days on end before he brought back a bit of meat for the pot.

One day, Jacob was just sitting down to eat a plate of his mother's bean stew when Esau arrived home.

"That smells good!" exclaimed Esau, dropping a dead deer on the floor. "I'm starving! Got any to spare?"

"Sorry," said Jacob. "There's only enough for one. You'll be eating later," he added, nodding toward the deer.

"It'll be hours before that's ready."

Jacob took another spoonful of the stew, rolling the taste around on his tongue. "What would you give me for it?" he asked.

"Anything!" said Esau.

"Even your birthright?"

"My birthright?"

"Your right to be head of the tribe after Isaac. As well as the flocks, herds, tents, and everything."

"I'd swap it all right now for a dish of that stew."

"No, you wouldn't," said Jacob calmly.

"I would! If I don't eat this minute, I'll die of hunger. A fat lot of good all the flocks, herds, and tents will be to me then!"

"All right." Jacob got up and pushed the dish toward him: "It's a bargain. I'll go and make myself some more."

Esau dug into his bean stew without another thought about his birthright.

But Rebecca remembered. It was one more black mark against Esau. What an idiot! He wasn't fit to be head of the tribe!

Time went by.

They all grew older. Isaac was quite blind now and hardly ever left his bed.

Rebecca never told him how Esau had swapped his birthright for a dish of bean stew. Isaac would have said it was just a joke, that it didn't mean anything. It was the blessing that counted. Once he'd given his solemn blessing to Esau, Esau would be head of the tribe. Rebecca knew that time was near.

There was not much the old man enjoyed now, but he did still like a meal of venison.

One day, as Esau was leaving for the hunt, Isaac called him in. "Bring home a deer," he said, "and cook it for me the way I like it. This is a special occasion."

From the way he spoke, Rebecca knew that when Esau brought him that dish of venison, the old man was going to give him his blessing.

"Quickly now," she said to Jacob. "Go out

and kill two young goats from the herd. I'll cook them so your father won't know them from venison."

When the meat was stewing nicely, she said, "Now, go and fetch your brother's best clothes and put them on."

"They smell," said Jacob.

"That's the idea," said Rebecca. "You'll smell like Esau."

Jacob shook his head: "This won't work. Esau's hands are hairy. Mine are smooth."

"I've thought of that," said Rebecca. She took bits of the goatskins and tied them over Jacob's hands and around the back of his neck, where Esau's hair grew long and ragged.

She pushed the dish of meat into his hands: "There! Off you go and claim your birthright."

Rebecca was the sort of mother who doesn't take "Don't want to!" for an answer. Jacob took the dish and went.

Isaac's head turned toward the sound of the curtain being brushed aside. There was nothing wrong with his hearing or his sense of smell. "It that you, Esau?" His face brightened.

"Yes," said Jacob, trying to make his voice sound deeper, like Esau's.

Then Isaac smelled the meat: "My!" he exclaimed. "You've been quick. Come over here and sit down. I want to hear all about the hunt."

"It was just a hunt like any other," mumbled Jacob.

"What's the matter with your voice? Aren't

you well? Give me your hand."

Jacob was glad of the goatskins covering it as he let Isaac hold his hand.

"The meat is getting cold," he said.

"Yes, yes," said Isaac, patting him on the shoulder, feeling the long hair at his neck.

All the time, Jacob was listening for the sound of the huntsmen coming back. If his father once heard Esau's voice outside, he'd know it was a trick and he would curse him, not bless him. But the night was quiet.

When the old man had eaten, he gave to Jacob the blessing which should have been Esau's and all of his inheritance, flocks, herds, tents, and all. No one could take it away, not even Isaac himself.

Why shouldn't I have it? Jacob said to himself. Esau didn't want it. He agreed to swap. His birthright for a dish of bean stew!

"Now," said Isaac, "tell me about the hunt."

There was no reply. He was alone.

Jacob flung off his borrowed clothes and crept away to hide. He listened for the roar of rage that would tell him Esau had found out how he had been cheated. Esau's rages were terrible, though they never lasted long.

He waited and waited. But it was Rebecca who came looking for him.

"The birthright is yours," she said. "No one can take it away from you, but they're both very angry. I think you should go away for a while. Go north, to your Uncle Laban, who lives in Padan-Aram."

So Jacob traveled north, meaning only to stay for a little while. It turned out to be more than twenty years. It was not long after arriving in Padan-Aram that Jacob fell in love with his cousin Rachel, but at first her father wouldn't hear of them marrying. It was all very well, Laban said, to talk of an inheritance waiting for him, but would he ever dare go home and collect it?

In the end, they struck a bargain. If Jacob

would work for Laban for seven years, then he could marry Rachel.

So he did.

It wasn't until after the wedding that he realized Laban had cheated him. He lifted up his bride's veil and there was not Rachel, but her elder sister, Leah.

Laban just shrugged his shoulders. "What was I to do?" he said. "If the younger sister marries first, the older one never gets a husband. I'll make a bargain with you: work another seven years and you can have Rachel, too."

Jacob was a lot like his mother, determined to get what he wanted.

"All right," he said.

After another seven years, he finally married the girl he loved.

Jacob became a very rich man: if there was one thing he knew about, it was livestock farming. But he missed his home and his brother Esau, whom he had tricked out of his birthright all those years ago.

The time came for him to make peace with Esau, if he could. So he rounded up his flocks and herds, packed up his tents, and off they all went.

Of course, a party that size can't go very far without people noticing. News ran ahead of them.

Word came back that Esau was coming to meet them with four hundred men.

Jacob looked around at his precious herds, the women, and the children. What could he do to calm his brother's anger?

I'll send him presents—lots of presents!

He started picking out the best of his flock and sending them ahead in little groups. He'll see I'm really sorry—I only want to be friends.

Still Esau and his four hundred men came on, until the two parties were camped within sight of one another.

Slowly the two brothers walked out alone

for their first meeting in—how many years?

This is it, thought Jacob. This is the moment I've been afraid of since that night I cheated Father into giving me his blessing.

It was hard to read the expression on Esau's face under the hair and the beard. That much hadn't changed.

All Jacob could see were the eyes, shining unnaturally bright. What with? Anger? Laughter? Tears! There were tears in Esau's eyes as he grabbed Jacob in a bearhug and lifted him clean off his feet.

"Oh, little brother!" roared Esau. "It's good to see you!" He gestured to the men behind him. "They all had to come and welcome you back. I couldn't persuade any of them to stay behind. There are just a few boys looking after the flocks, but I think you'll find they're all there."

Jacob looked at him in amazement: "You're not angry with me anymore?"

Esau laughed again: "I never was. We made a bargain. And I think I got the best of it. You got more than twenty years in exile. I got the best bowl of bean stew I ever tasted."

THE DREAMER OF DREAMS

Joseph was a dreamer. Not a head-in-the-clouds sort of dreamer. Joseph's dreams had meaning, or so it seemed to his father, Jacob.

Joseph dreamed a dream in which he was harvesting barley along with his brothers. And all their sheaves of barley bowed down before his.

He dreamed a dream in which he was a star in the sky and all the other stars bowed down before him, and the sun and the moon as well.

It was clear to Jacob what the dreams meant. Joseph was someone special, favored by God. Though Joseph was the eleventh of his twelve sons, Joseph was to be head of the family after him.

While his brothers worked for their keep, tending the flocks of sheep and goats, Joseph

48

was kept at home studying. His brothers wore robes of brown and gray, the color of the land they lived on. But Jacob dressed Joseph in a coat of many colors. Poppy red. Flax blue. The green of meadows after spring rain . . .

Of course his brothers were jealous. Who wouldn't be? As soon as the old man was out of the way, they scoffed at Joseph, the idler, the dreamer, in his fancy coat.

"What does he look like?"

"Like a rooster strutting in the henyard."

"Ooh! My eyes! I'm dazzled! I think I've gone blind!"

"Don't let him near the sheep. He'll cause a stampede!"

Only Benjamin, the youngest, whispered so no one could hear: "I think it's beautiful, Joseph."

"Do you want to try it on?" Joseph offered.

Benjamin looked doubtful: "Later, perhaps. When there's no one to see."

When the elder brothers left to herd the sheep up to the summer pastures, Benjamin stayed behind because he was the youngest. But Joseph stayed home too, only because Jacob wanted it that way. Then the old man began to fret: "I hope everything's all right." He decided to send Joseph after them, just to make sure they were safe.

Off went Joseph in his many-colored coat.

When the brothers saw that coat in the distance they thought at first it must be a mirage. Or else a bad dream.

There they were, hot and tired from herding and shearing and worrying about the poor grazing this year.

And here was Joseph, fresh as a posy of summer flowers.

"Your highness!" they exclaimed.

"What brings you to our humble abode?"

"We are not worthy!"

"Such an honor!"

Some of them bowed down before him (well, it was in his dream, wasn't it?), others groveled on their knees in the dust, then picked it up in handfuls and threw it at him.

They pushed him and jostled him, spun him round and knocked him down, pulled off his pretty coat and tried it on for size.

They held a Josephlook-alike competition:

"Look at me! I'm Joseph."

"No! This is Joseph! He walks like this . . ."

Each one grabbing at the many colored coat, until Reuben, the eldest, shouted: "That's enough!"

Slowly they all came to their senses and saw the beautiful coat lying torn and trampled in the dust.

"What's Father going to say?"

"We won't tell him."

"I'll have to tell him," said Joseph.

"We're not going to have you telling tales."

"We're sick of you lording it over us!"

Some of them drew their knives. "It's time to put a stop to it for good!"

"Don't be stupid," said Reuben. "We can't kill our own brother."

"What shall we do, then?"

"I don't know," said Reuben. "I need time to think."

"Be quick about it. We don't want our little rooster running home to crow the news from the housetops."

"Let's throw him down that dry well to cool off," suggested Reuben.

So they lowered Joseph down the well and Reuben went off on his own to tend the sheep. Later, when the others weren't around, he planned to let Joseph go.

But when he got back, he found the nine brothers sitting quietly around the empty well.

"Where's Joseph?" asked Reuben. "What have you done?"

"Joseph?" said Judah. "He should be well on his way to Egypt by now." He tossed Reuben two silver coins. "That's your share."

"We got twenty for him," Simeon explained. "That's two each."

"There were these merchants . . ." said Levi.

". . . who just happened to be passing through," grinned Judah.

"What are we going to tell them at home?" demanded Reuben.

Levi held up the coat of many colors, now stained with the blood of a newly-killed lamb.

"Our poor little brother must have got himself eaten by some nasty wild animal. Oh dear. What is poor father going to say? But it's not our fault, is it? . . . That lamb should be cooked by now. Come on. Let's eat."

JOSEPH IN EGYPT

In Egypt, things didn't go so badly at first for Joseph.

He had been sold as a slave, to a man named Potiphar, but he made the best of things and he worked so well that he was soon running Potiphar's household.

Then he disagreed with Potiphar's wife. She told lies about him to her husband and without checking to find out if they were true, Potiphar had Joseph flung into jail. No trial, no sentence. He might be there for the rest of his life. Still, Joseph made the best of things.

Among the Egyptians, a dreamer of dreams —a man who could tell you what your dreams meant, as Joseph could—was a man everyone respected. Prisoners came to him looking for help and advice:

"I had this dream last night. Can you tell me what it means?"

"How long before I'm out of this place?"

"Tell me my future! Is it good or bad?"

But after they were released, they never remembered Joseph. They wanted to forget about their time in jail.

Then Pharaoh himself started having bad dreams.

All the Egyptians went about with worried faces. The way they looked at it, Pharaoh *was* Egypt. If Pharaoh was having bad dreams, that meant hard times ahead for the whole country.

The worst of it was that nobody—out of all the hundreds of priests and magicians and wise men who surrounded him—could tell him what the dreams meant.

Then the man who poured the wine for him at dinner whispered: "There is a young Hebrew in the royal prison who can tell the meaning of dreams. He told me I would be released and pardoned three days before it happened."

"Amazing!" said Pharaoh. "I didn't know it myself then."

"At the same time, he told your baker that he would be hanged."

"That was already decided. The man was guilty. But fetch this Hebrew. Let's see what he has to say."

Joseph had already heard about Pharaoh's dream. Everyone in Egypt had heard it by now. In the markets and the taverns they were all trying to work it out.

But he stood patiently, while Pharaoh told the dream over again, in case there was anything the gossips had missed.

"I dreamed," said Pharaoh, "that I was standing by the Nile River, when out of the

river came seven fine, fat cows. Sleek, well fed, prime beef cattle, every one. Then after them, out of the water, came seven more. But they were poor starving creatures, their sides caved in with hunger, almost too weak to stand.

56

Yet these seven thin cows ate the seven fat ones and still remained as thin as before. That was all my dream and I can make no sense of it."

Joseph smiled to himself: God had already given him the answer. The key to it was the Nile River. On either side of Egypt the desert sand stretched far beyond the horizon, but Egypt is the Gift of the Nile. Every year the river floods, watering the land and laying down fresh, fertile soil. No flood, no harvest.

"So," said Joseph, "the seven fat cows are seven good harvests, which will be followed by seven bad—so bad, it will seem as though the good years had never been."

All the wise men standing around Pharaoh looked grave and nodded their heads: why, yes, of course!

"How am I going to feed my people through seven years of famine?" asked Pharaoh.

The wise men said nothing.

"God has shown you the way," said Joseph. "You have seven good years to prepare. Build special royal warehouses. Save part of the harvest each year and when the bad times come, share what you have saved fairly among the people."

There was only one man to oversee that job. That morning Joseph had been a prisoner. By evening he was Governor of Egypt.

A hard time he had of it, for seven long years, traveling up and down the land of Egypt, persuading the people to part with one-fifth of everything they grew.

Then the seven lean years began and the work was even harder, always keeping an eye open, in case the storekeepers took a bit extra for their families or to sell on the black market.

It seemed as if the whole world was in the grip of the famine.

Foreigners came from Canaan and from Midian, from Edom and from Moab, to buy what Egypt had to spare.

Joseph had to set a fair price and see to it that none of them were cheated.

Then one day among the crowd he saw a face he recognized.

Judah!

His beard was thicker now, with streaks of gray, but it was his brother Judah. No doubt about it.

Quickly Joseph's eyes scanned the crowd and picked out Reuben . . . Levi . . . Simeon . . . How rough and dirty they all looked to someone who'd spent more than half his life in Pharaoh's court!

"Have those men brought to me," said Joseph.

In vain he looked for Benjamin.

Soon the rest stood before him, ten brothers, picked out of the crowd by this Egyptian magician.

How did he know they were brothers? What did he want?

They bowed their heads. Not one of them dared look him in the eye for long enough to recognize their long lost brother.

"Why have you come to Egypt?" Joseph asked in his most princely manner.

Reuben answered: "Lord, we are the sons of Jacob. We've come to Egypt to buy food, because there is no food in Canaan."

"I think you're lying," said Joseph. "I think you're spies come to seek out our weak points, so you can mount a raid across the border."

"No, lord. We're honest farmers. Our father, Jacob, is well-known in Canaan."

"But are you all his sons?"

The brothers looked at one another.

Reuben spoke again: "We are ten of twelve. The youngest is at home. The other . . ."

". . . is dead," said Judah. "Years ago."

Joseph looked thoughtful. "Bring me this

young brother of yours," he said, "and I'll believe you. One of you must remain here as a hostage. The rest will go and fetch him."

He was tempted to pick Judah to stay in Egypt. A spell in the state prison would do him good. But he chose Simeon instead.

The others made their way home, worried and puzzled.

They were even more puzzled when they got there and opened up the bags of food they'd brought from Egypt. In the top of each one was the money they were supposed to have paid for it. What was this Egyptian up to?

Whatever it was, old Jacob didn't like it. He flatly refused to let them take Benjamin to Egypt.

Poor Benjamin. Since Joseph went, he'd hardly been allowed out of his father's sight. He would have seized the chance to see a bit more of the world.

And what about Simeon, left behind in Egypt?

Simeon must take his chance.

Time went by and the famine showed no sign of ending.

The food from Egypt was all gone.

"We must go back," Judah told his father, "or all the family will starve. But we dare not go without Benjamin. I'll take care of him, I swear it."

At last the old man gave in. He gave them the price of the first lot of corn to take with them and money to buy more. He gave them gifts for this strange Egyptian—oils and spices, scents and sandalwood, the best he could afford.

But when they were brought before him – not in the warehouse this time, but in his own palace—the Egyptian barely glanced at his presents.

When they said that they were sorry about

the mix-up with the money—they'd never meant to take the corn without paying for it— he didn't seem to hear them. He just stared at their faces one after the other, ending with Benjamin.

"How is your father?" he said at last.

"He's well," said Benjamin.

Joseph felt his eyes filling with tears.

Quickly he got up and left the room. In his own apartments, he cried and cried.

The brothers stood where he'd left them, bewildered.

Then servants came to fetch them—"This way, sirs, if you please,"—leading them to where hot baths were waiting for them, and afterward fresh clothes and a banquet such as men who've lived through years of famine dream of every night.

Benjamin's plate was piled far higher than the others. If some of the food was the sort of thing that used to be his favorite when he was little, that was just one more odd thing among all the rest.

The following day they set off on the journey home, taking Simeon along with them. He'd been treated well and was almost sorry to be going home.

They'd barely crossed the border when they heard the galloping of hooves behind them.

"What is it?" asked Reuben. "What's the matter?"

"There is a thief among you."

"No!"

The guards unloaded the sacks of food.

In each one, as before, the money lay. The guards weren't interested in that.

At last they came to Benjamin, slashed open the sacks his donkey carried and found what they were looking for. A jeweled silver cup.

"My master's cup! The one that Pharaoh gave him. The one he uses for telling fortunes."

"I didn't take it," said Benjamin. "I've never seen it before."

"The rest of you can go," said the guard. "He comes with us."

"If he goes back," said Reuben, "then we all do."

So back they went.

There they stood again before this strange Egyptian, the cup produced in evidence against them and no explanation as to how it could have got into Benjamin's sack of corn. It was Joseph himself who had had it put there, of course, but that thought never entered their heads.

"I will be merciful," said Joseph. "The rest of you can go. Benjamin stays, as my slave."

Then Judah stepped forward.

"Lord," he said. "I don't know how the cup got there, but my brother is no thief. He is our father's youngest son. Years ago, when he thought Joseph was dead, the shock almost killed him. But Joseph didn't die. I sold him into slavery. If anyone deserves to be a slave, it's me. Take me in Benjamin's place."

All this was news to Benjamin. He'd always thought Joseph was dead. Now a host of little things all fell into place.

He stared at Joseph. Joseph stared back and suddenly he could bear the pretence no longer.

"Joseph is not dead," he said.

Benjamin cried: "It's you, isn't it? Joseph! You idiots, can't you see?"

Then Joseph hugged them all, one by one, beginning with Benjamin and ending with Judah.

"I have one more dream," he told them. "One I dream often. There is a piece of land in the North. A place called Goshen, just right for grazing sheep and goats. I dream of seeing our family settle there. Go home and fetch our father, Jacob. Tell him the land of Goshen is his and his children's, and his children's children's . . ."

And it wasn't long before that dream came true, too.

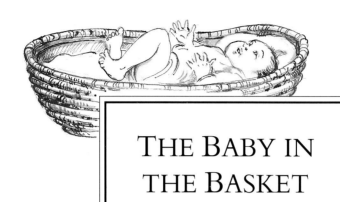

THE BABY IN THE BASKET

More than anything in the world, Miriam wanted a baby brother.

"You've got me," said Aaron. "I'm your brother."

"You're just a boy," said Miriam.

"I was a baby once."

"I suppose you were. I don't remember."

"Neither do I," said Aaron. "Anyway, you'd better start hoping the new baby's a girl, because if it's a boy, they're going to kill it."

"They're what? Who?"

Aaron shrugged. "People. I don't know."

"People don't kill babies!" exclaimed Miriam.

Of course she didn't believe him. Well, perhaps she half-believed him. There enough of a niggling doubt in her mind for her to tell her father, Amram, what Aaron had said.

"It's not true, is it?" said Miriam.

"I'm afraid it is true," said Amram quietly. "If the new baby turns out to be a boy, then he'll be taken away from us and killed."

"Who by?"

"The Egyptians. We're Israelites, living in their country. They welcomed us once, but now they say there are too many of us. So the Pharoah has passed a law saying that all our baby boys are to be killed. Just pray for a little sister."

Miriam didn't want a sister. She wanted a baby brother so badly that it hurt.

And the baby was a boy.

His mother, Jochebed, began to cry when she saw him and she went on crying as if she never meant to stop. Aaron and Amram went about with long faces. They knew it was just a matter of time before the soldiers came to take the baby away.

Miriam thought and thought about how they could save her new baby brother. The best time for thinking was when she was down by the river, cutting reeds.

Jochebed used the reeds to make all sorts of things: mats to sleep on and shades to keep out the sun; hats and shoes and belts and baskets. It took a lot of reeds, but they cost nothing, except the time it took to cut them, standing up to your knees in water, keeping a sharp look-out for crocodiles.

Miriam had found the perfect place, near where Pharaoh's daughter came down to bathe each day. No danger of crocodiles here. The princess's guards would have seen to that. If a crocodile came within a mile of the princesses, the guard who missed it would have been crocodile meat in about as much time as it took to throw him in.

Sometimes while Miriam was working there, the Pharaoh's daughter and her maids came down to bathe. Miriam could hear them splashing and laughing. Sometimes she watched them, keeping her head down, pretending to be busy with her work. Once she looked up and saw the princess smiling at her. She looked nice.

I wonder what she thinks about them killing babies? Miriam thought. I wonder what she'd do if it were *her* baby brother?

She gathered up all the reeds she'd cut, twisted two of them into a rope and used them to tie the rest of the bundle. Then she carried the bundle home on her head.

All her ideas seemed to be fitting themselves into place, the way things do if you worry about a problem long enough.

Jochebed was sitting in the shade weaving a basket. She worked so fast and pulled the reeds so tight, that her baskets would hold water right to the brim and never spill a drop.

"I've got an idea," whispered Miriam. "A way to save the baby." Very, very softly she whispered in Jochebed's ear.

For the first time in days Jochebed smiled.

She began to work the basket into a different shape.

"Why are you making it that funny shape?" asked Aaron.

"It's a secret," said Miriam.

Jochebed said softly. "It's for the baby. I'm making him a little cradle out of rushes."

That night the baby slept soundly, all tucked up in his new little bed.

Miriam didn't sleep a wink.

Before dawn she was up and dressed. But

Jochebed was up before her. Quietly, so as not to wake the baby, she gave him one last kiss. Then Miriam picked up the cradle and slipped out of the house. Dawn found her crouched in the reed bed, with the cradle bobbing up and down on the water beside her.

Time passed.

She heard the crocodile patrol go up the river and heard them come back again.

Still she waited. She could feel her toes going all wrinkly from being so long in the water.

The baby was being very good, considering he'd had no breakfast. He lay watching the sunlight dancing on the reeds, the clouds chasing one another across the sky, and the dragonflies darting to and fro.

At last they came, the princess and her maids, crying out because the water was cold.

"Good luck, little brother," whispered Miriam.

She pushed the cradle out into the river and watched it float away.

A few minutes later she heard their excited voices:

"What is it? What have you found?"

"You'll never believe me. Look for yourself."

"A baby! Oh, he's beautiful!"

"Where did it come from?"

"Isn't it obvious?" A new voice, cold and harsh: "It's one of the Israelite babies. Ugh! Nasty little thing! Throw it back! Let the crocodiles have it!"

That couldn't be the princess! Could it?

In a moment, Miriam was out of the water and running along the bank, ready to dive in and save her brother if she had to.

It wasn't the princess who'd spoken. The princess was taking the baby, smiling, letting him play with her necklace.

"He's just a baby," she said. "Anyway, how

do you know it's an Israelite baby?"

"By the cloth that it's wrapped in," said the sour-faced girl.

"By the weave of the basket—the same as the shoes that child is carrying."

Miriam quickly hid her sandals behind her back.

The princess smiled down at the baby. "How can anyone kill a baby? They shan't kill you, little baby. You're mine now. I shall call you Moses."

"Ra-moses?" one of the maids suggested. "Son-of-the-god-Ra?"

"I like Tut-moses, son of Thoth," said another.

"What do you think?" the princess asked Miriam.

"I don't know," said Miriam. "Our God doesn't have a name."

"Just Moses, then?"

"All right."

Then little Moses came close to spoiling everything by beginning to cry. He didn't just cry: he bawled. He held his breath and turned scarlet. Then he bawled some more.

"I think he's hungry," said Miriam. "He's had no breakfast—at least, I don't expect so."

"Do you know anyone who could feed him?" shouted the princess above the din.

"There's an Israelite woman called Jochebed who had a baby not long ago."

"Fetch her!" the princess cried, and Miriam went running off.

Soon Jochebed came.

Moses stopped crying the moment she took him from the princess.

Soon he was quietly feeding and it was possible to talk.

"Her baby was a boy, too," Miriam whispered to the princess.

"Oh!" The princess nodded.

"We don't know where this one came from, do we?" said Miriam more loudly. "But I think the princess is going to adopt him," she said to Jochebed.

Jochebed said nothing. She smiled down at the baby.

"I shall need a nurse for him," said the princess. "Will you look after him for me?"

Jochebed nodded. She couldn't speak. She was too busy smiling and crying all at the same time.

"His name is Moses," said Miriam.

Very softly, she whispered to herself, so no one else could hear: "My baby brother, Moses."

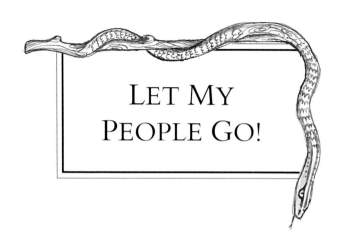

LET MY
PEOPLE GO!

Who am I?
What am I?

Am I a Hebrew or an Egyptian?

Over and over again Moses asked himself these questions.

He knew who his parents were. His parents were Hebrews, but he'd been brought up at the Egyptian court.

He wandered far away from Egypt, living among the desert tribes who welcomed him, as they did all strangers, and gave him food and shelter.

Sooner or later the question would come up. "Where are you from? Who are your people?"

"I am Moses," he said.

"Ah! An Egyptian."

"No. I am a Hebrew."

He found it easy to say, now that both nations were far away. One day as he traveled on alone he saw the strangest thing.

He thought at first it was just the heat-haze over the sand.

But at the heart of it there was a steady flickering of flame. As he came nearer, he saw that it was a bush on fire. But instead of crumbling into ashes, it just kept on burning, burning . . .

Some god was in this place, for sure.

He covered his head and kicked off his

shoes, though the sand scorched his bare feet.

From within the burning bush he heard a voice: "I am the One God. The God the Hebrews worshiped long before they came to Egypt. I have chosen you, Moses, to lead them out of Egypt, back to the land their fathers came from."

"Me?" Moses shook his head. "I'm no leader. I couldn't lead a flock of sheep to water. My brother Aaron, he's good with words . . ."

"Take Aaron with you when you go to see Pharaoh."

"Pharaoh hates me. He despises me. When we were little, he used to call me Little No-name. Nobody's Child. He'll never listen to me."

"You must make him listen. The message is, *Let my people go!*"

Before many days had passed, there was Moses standing before Pharaoh. On the one side, Pharaoh, in his embroidered robes, sitting on his golden throne, with all his courtiers and priests and magicians lined up behind him. On the other, Moses, still a bit dusty from the desert, with Aaron beside him.

"Well, well!" said Pharaoh. "If it isn't little No-name!"

"The God who protects me has no name," said Moses. "He is the One God. The only God."

"Really?" said Pharaoh. "So all these people —he meant the priests and magicians—have got it wrong, have they? And you're right."

"Yes," said Moses.

"Prove it," said Pharaoh. "Show me what your God can do."

Then at a sign from Moses, Aaron threw his staff on the floor and it became a snake.

Pharaoh yawned: "Oh, that old trick!" He snapped his fingers. At once, all the priests and magicians threw down their staffs and the floor became a writhing mass of snakes.

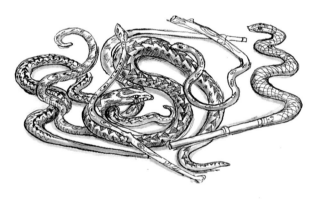

Everyone was too busy keeping out of the way at first to notice what was happening. The mass of snakes was getting smaller. Fewer and fewer. Aaron's snake was eating all the rest. When it had gobbled up the very last one, Moses picked it up by its tail and it turned back into a stick of wood.

Pharaoh was not amused. "And what does he want, this one God?"

"Let my people go," said Moses.

"Your people! You mean the Hebrews?"

"You don't like us. You're afraid of us. Let us go, out of Egypt, back to the land of our forefathers."

"Get rid of them?" exclaimed Pharaoh. "Just like that? I'd like to, Moses. But then, who would work in our stone quarries? And clear away the garbage? Who would build my great new city of Ramesses on the delta? Egyptians? I don't think so. Sorry, I can't help you."

Moses had made things no better for the Hebrews. In fact, Pharaoh saw to it that they got worse. More work, longer hours, and if they wanted to know whose fault it was, they need look no further than Moses.

But that wasn't the end of the story. It was hardly even the beginning.

Far, far to the south, it had begun to rain. Raining as it had never rained before, washing the red clay of the Sudan into the river.

One day when Pharaoh went down to the river for his daily swim, he saw Moses on the bank.

When he saw Pharaoh, Moses shouted out: "Will you let my people go?"

"No!" shouted Pharaoh.

Moses stretched out his staff over the waters as God had told him to.

Pharaoh looked down. Then he stepped back in horror. The water of the river was flowing blood red.

That was the beginning.

In the polluted waters, fish died in their thousands.

The frogs were better off. They could climb out of the water, onto the land.

And they did. Frogs everywhere. Frogs in the streets and in the houses. Upstairs and downstairs. In the pantry and under the bed, and in the bed.

The court magicians tried to save face.

"A plague of frogs?" they said. "Oh, yes! Anyone can do it."

"But can you stop it?" demanded Pharaoh.

They shook their heads.

Pharaoh sent for Moses. "Take off this

curse," he begged him.

"Will you let my people go?"

"It's what you want, isn't it?" Pharaoh was very careful not to say yes. He wasn't going to let them go, not after this!

Soon afterward the plague of flies began.

If Pharaoh hadn't tried to outsmart him, Moses might have given him some good advice about clearing up the dead frogs. The Egyptians had long ago forgotten how to sweep their own streets. This was work for Hebrews.

So the frogs just lay there festering, great heaps of them.

There's nothing flies enjoy more than a meal of rotting meat.

Mosquitoes, on the other hand, like to breed in stagnant water and there was plenty of that, too.

And, of course, there were the fleas and lice, because there was not enough clean water to wash in.

People lay sick in their houses and the cattle died in the fields.

But would Pharaoh let the Hebrews go? Never!

"God is angry," said Moses. "That is why He has sent these plagues to afflict you. Will you let us go into the desert to make a sacrifice to Him?"

"All of you?"

"All of us."

"Women and children, too? Babes in arms? You don't need to take them with you to make a sacrifice. And just how far into the desert were you planning to go?"

"A three days' journey."

Moses was offering him a way out. Send us into the desert to make our sacrifice. We just won't come back. You won't have given in, but we'll be gone. The suffering will stop.

Pharaoh understood what Moses was offering.

"No," he said.

Then the hailstorms began. Great lumps of ice, as big as your fist, able to strike dead any living creature that was left outside.

The Hebrews, of course, had had fair warning from Moses and Aaron, but the Egyptians had a hard time of it.

The storm clouds had barely cleared away

when the wind veered around to the east and a strange murmuring filled the air.

Locusts!

Millions of them.

The Egyptians took up sticks and flails, the women thrashed them with their shawls, but the winged insects were everywhere, stripping the trees leaf by leaf and destroying every last blade of grass. Then they were gone again, nothing but a distant humming in the air, leaving Egypt, the Gift of the Nile, a barren wasteland.

And still Pharaoh stood firm.

What more could God do? One thing more. The worst thing of all.

Moses went to Pharaoh and Pharaoh said, "You may go into the desert to sacrifice to your

God. Just the men. The women and children stay here."

Moses shook his head: "Not good enough. Listen to me."

"No." Pharaoh spread his arms wide. "What more can your God do?"

"Pharaoh, do you love your son? For his sake, let my people go. For his sake and the sake of all the eldest sons of Egypt."

"Do you dare to threaten my son?" roared Pharaoh. "Get out of my sight! If you come here again, I'll kill you!"

Sadly Moses went away to give Aaron his instructions to pass on to the Hebrews:

"Get ready to leave. But first, one last meal. Roast lamb with bitter herbs. Take some of the blood of the lamb and smear it around the door. Then stay inside. No one must go out for any reason until morning."

No one slept. Even the tiniest babies lay quietly, eyes wide open, as if they could hear the beating of great wings passing overhead.

The Angel of Death moved on toward the homes of the Egyptians.

Soon after midnight, they heard the first scream of terror and disbelief.

Then another.

And another, until the whole of Egypt was mourning its sons.

From the prisoner in the dungeon, to Pharaoh in his palace, the first born son of every family was dead, all in a single night.

It was, as God had promised, the worst thing of all.

"Take your accursed people," Pharaoh screamed, "and go! Before I slaughter every last one of you and wipe you from the face of the earth! And what will your no-name god do then, with no one left to worship him?"

The Hebrews had their things packed ready for the journey.

Out of their houses they came in their hundreds, in their thousands, saying a quick prayer of thanks, and another for a safe journey.

Where were they going?

Nobody quite knew. A land their fathers and their grandfathers had told them of when they were very young. A land where dreams came true and everyone was happy and the rivers flowed with milk and honey.

Which way? Which way?

Follow Moses. God will show him the way.

When will we get there?

This year?

Next year?

Sometime.

Maybe never.

They hadn't been going for much more than a day when they began to wonder whether this was such a good idea after all. The hard time they'd been having in Egypt was nothing to what they were having to put up with now. At least in Egypt if they wanted a drink of water all they had to do was fetch it from the well. At least they didn't have to sleep on the cold, hard ground under the stars.

The small children were whining and demanding to be carried and the bigger ones kept falling behind and getting lost.

Who was this Moses anyway?

Aaron, they trusted. Aaron, they knew. But they could see now that Aaron was taking all his orders from Moses. Did Moses really know where he was taking them?

Then they came to the sea—a long arm of water, stretching far inland; farther than anyone could see, never mind walk around. Standing on the sand, they could just make out the distant shore. But there was no way across—unless, for his next trick, Moses was going to teach them all to walk on water?

"Trick?" muttered Moses. "Just a few tricks! Is that what they think of all I've done so far?"

"All *I've* done," God reminded him.

"Sorry," said Moses.

"It happens all the time," said God. "People have a very short memory for miracles."

Including Pharaoh. Yes, Pharaoh had taken just twenty-four hours to get over the death of his son. Now he was on the move, with his army and his chariots, to fetch those Hebrews back again. He would not be beaten by Nobody's Child and his no-name god!

It wasn't hard to see which way they'd gone. All those thousands of feet had raised a dust-cloud you could see for miles. Now the Hebrews were trapped between the Egyptians and the sea.

"We'll camp for the night," decided Pharaoh. "Let the dust settle and attack in the morning."

All night Moses prayed for God to help them.

By morning everything had changed.

To say the tide had gone out would be to put it mildly. The sea was nothing but a glittering of sunlight on a distant wall of water and the far-off roaring of a mighty monster demanding to be set free.

Ahead was nothing but wet sand, tiny rock-pools, shellfish and seaweed, scuttling crabs, and probably quicksand, too.

"Quickly, then," said God to Moses. "You haven't got much time."

Moses stepped onto the shifting sands.

"Is it safe?" he wondered.

"Quickly, I said. Keep moving. Don't stop."

After Moses came Aaron.

Some of the children followed them onto the squelchy sand, watching their footsteps form and fade. Their mothers went to fetch them back, glanced over their shoulders at the Egyptians, and decided to press on. Between the Egyptians and the deep blue sea, they'd rather take their chances with the sea.

Soon all the Hebrews were on the move. Nobody spoke. They kept glancing fearfully at the distant wall of water, which seemed to be growing taller. The roaring of the monster, ever-louder.

"What are you waiting for?" screamed Pharaoh. "After them! Where they can go, so can we."

The men might have been ready to obey him, but the horses were not. They could hear the roaring. They could smell the salt spray. They bucked and reared and tried to turn back.

As soon as the chariots stopped, their narrow wheels began to sink into the sand. Foot soldiers, already sinking ankle-deep in their heavy armor, stopped to help pull the chariots free and only sank deeper themselves.

And all the time, the monster roared and fought to break free.

As the last of the Hebrews stepped onto dry land, the sea swept down on Pharaoh's army.

In a few seconds they were up to their knees . . . their waists . . . their shoulders . . .

Then it was all over. An army lay buried beneath the tumbling waters, as though it had never existed.

There was no going back now. The Hebrews turned away from the tumbling waves and waited for Moses to lead them.

"They will follow you now," said God, "wherever you go."

"All the way to the Promised Land?"

"All the way."

ONE MAN AND HIS DONKEY

His name was Balaam and he was a small-time prophet.

Very small-time. The prophecies came few and far between. He got by with a bit of weather forecasting, herbal remedies, and generally giving good advice.

Curses he didn't do as a rule. Curses had a nasty way of bouncing back if you weren't very, very careful. But if someone lost something valuable and they suspected it might have been stolen, it was fairly safe to put a curse out on the thief if he didn't put the thing back. Most of the objects turned up quite soon afterward. The rest were probably just lost, and lost for good.

One day two very important visitors came up the narrow path to the cave where Balaam lived.

People expected a prophet to live in a cave. It showed he wasn't interested in worldly things. Actually it was a lot more comfortable than some houses. Warm in winter and cool in summer, with plenty of room for himself and his donkey.

Up the path they came, these two fine fellows, trying hard to look dignified, while they clung to the litters they were being carried on. Any sensible person would have got off and walked, but they were much too grand.

They were messengers from the king himself.

"The king has a job for you."

"A job that can only be done by someone with your skill at cursing."

"You've had some good results, we hear."

Balaam tried to look modest. "I can only curse people who really deserve it."

"Oh, these people deserve it."

"It's more than one person, then?"

"Oh, yes!"

"Hundreds!"

Gradually, while their servants fanned them cool and washed their feet and poured them cups of refreshing wine, the two envoys explained that there was a tribe of desert-dwellers camped right on the borders of their kingdom.

That was nothing new. There was always some desert tribe or other raiding across the border, especially at this time of year.

Balaam frowned. "Sounds more like a job for the army," he said.

"The army's there."

"Been there for days with nothing to do."

"No battle to fight."

"It makes them nervous."

"All those Israelites, just sitting there."

"As if they're waiting for something."

"So the king thought if you could give them a good cursing . . ."

". . . they might go and sit somewhere else."

It didn't sound like a very good reason for cursing somebody. What if all the curses bounced back at him, hundreds of them, all at once? Balaam had a rule in cases like this: Never be too hasty.

"Come back in the morning," he said.

All night long he prayed and meditated. He burned sticks of incense. He stared into a lighted candle until the flame burned down and went out.

The message was very clear: Don't go!

But when they came back in the morning, the envoys were very persuasive. They offered him money—more money than he'd ever seen in his life. They offered him a place at court. He'd never have to live in this drafty old cave again.

Actually Balaam quite liked his cave.

They said he'd be famous.

Balaam decided it wouldn't do any harm to just go and look at these Israelites.

"I'm not making any promises, mind," he said, as he waved them off down the path.

He saddled his donkey and set off after them, still pondering the problem, letting the donkey find the way.

The donkey was a simple soul. Simple souls often see what's right in front of them when wise men are too busy looking at the far horizon.

Suddenly the donkey stopped. Balaam went on all by himself. He did a neat somersault over her head and ended up sitting on the ground in front of her.

He got up and thrashed her and at last he got her moving again, but she wouldn't follow the road. She'd decided to go the pretty way, it seemed, straight across country, with Balaam yelling at her and pulling on the reins, until they came to the next village.

For a while she was quiet again, walking through the village streets as quiet as a lamb.

Then all at once, she started rubbing herself up against a rough stone wall, as if Balaam were a nasty itch she was trying to scratch. He tore his robe and scraped his knee before he managed to wriggle free.

Look at the state of him! And him off to see the king!

She was usually such a good little donkey.

He beat her again, which made him late, so when they set off again he took a short cut along a narrow path between high cliffs. Just room enough for a donkey to squeeze through.

Would you believe it! She stopped again. She simply sat down.

Balaam slid gently down over her tail and landed on the ground behind her.

He was going to give her such a beating now! He lifted up his staff . . .

Then the donkey spoke: "I wish you wouldn't keep doing that," she said. "I've been your faithful servant since the day you bought me. But I'm not walking through fire for you or anyone."

Balaam was astonished: "You can talk?"

"I can talk," said the donkey. "And I can see what's right in front of my nose. Didn't you see the angel?"

"What angel?" asked Balaam.

"What angel? he says. Head in the clouds, now he's been sent for by the king. Sort of a fireball. Man with a flaming sword. Twice I've just managed to get us past, but this time there's no room. Can't you see it?"

Balaam screwed up his eyes and squinted into the sun.

There did seem to be something there. A sort of shimmering. A sort of glow, spreading wider, and in the center of it the figure of a man, arms outstretched, flames running to his fingers' ends; hair like cold fire . . .

"Do you get the feeling he's trying to tell you something?" the donkey said.

"I think we'd better go back," said Balaam.

"No!" said the figure. "It's too late to turn back now. You must go on."

Then a cloud passed over the face of the sun and the figure disappeared.

On they went to the king's camp.

"Everything's ready," said the king. "We've made the proper sacrifices. You can get on with the cursing straight away. I've picked out a good spot for it."

Balaam followed the king to the top of a hill, still looking nervously around in case the angel popped up again.

"There you are," said the king: "the Israelites!"

Balaam stared down at the Israelite camp. There weren't hundreds of them. There were thousands. They far outnumbered the king's army. And that was just the men. They'd brought their wives and children, their flocks and herds as well. These weren't raiders, they were settlers, coming in from the hard wandering life of the desert to make themselves a home.

"Go on," said the king. "Curse them."

Balaam faced the Israelites and spread his arms wide. It suddenly occurred to him that with the sun behind him he must look very like that figure he'd seen. The sun was a fiery halo behind his head and he could feel the warmth of it spreading across his back and down his arms to his fingers' ends.

All at once he understood what he had to do. Balaam was inspired. He just let the words come. He wished afterward he could have

remembered some of it, because it was the best bit of prophesying he'd ever done in his life.

The Israelites seemed pleased with it. It seemed to be just what they'd been waiting for. They began packing up their things, ready to move.

The king was furious, jumping up and down in a very unkingly way. "I told you to curse them, not bless them!" he yelled.

"They're moving, aren't they?" said Balaam.

"They're moving in!"

"I'm afraid that's prophecy for you. If the Israelites are destined to settle the land of Canaan, then they will settle it, no matter what you or your army do. Why don't you make them welcome? There's plenty of land for all."

With that, Balaam got on his donkey and rode away.

After they'd been going for a while, Balaam said: "This isn't the way home."

"Home," said the donkey, "is not a good idea at the moment. Home is where the king's going to come looking for you when everything goes wrong."

"I gave him good advice," said Balaam.

"Ah, but will he take it?" said the donkey.

"I don't suppose so," said Balaam.

"And humans call *us* stupid and stubborn," sighed the donkey. "Which way now?"

"You choose," said Balaam. "I really think you know best."

OUT OF THE STRONG, SOMETHING SWEET

It was dark in the prison cell. By night, as dark as the grave. By day, a faint light managed to struggle through a small window high up in the wall, but gave up before it reached the floor. Rats scuffled and squeaked in the shadows like lost souls, abandoned between this world and the next.

Light or dark, day or night, it was all one to the man. The man was blind.

Nobody cared what the boy felt or thought. He was less than nothing. The slave of a slave.

"Here's your new dog, Samson," the guard had said, pushing the boy ahead of him into the cell.

In the dim light of the lantern, the boy could

see what looked like a bundle of filthy rags lying in a corner.

The guard went over and kicked it. Slowly the bundle sat up and turned itself into a man. Thin as a scarecrow he was, the bones sticking through his flesh, his hair hacked off short as a worn scrub brush. He had empty sockets where his eyes should have been.

The guard was already backing away: "I said, here's your new dog, Samson. Don't eat him like you did the last one."

Safe on the other side of the door, he added, "Samson, the mighty hero. The strongest man in the world, they used to say. He doesn't look such a big man now, does he?"

"But he's still frightened of me," murmured Samson. "Has he gone?"

The boy nodded, forgetting the man could not see.

"So you're my new dog. Come here."

The boy stayed where he was.

"It's all right. I won't really eat you. I don't eat children. Even Philistine ones. Are you a Philistine?"

The boy shook his head.

"It doesn't matter, either way. What's your name?"

No answer. He'd had a name once, but he'd long ago forgotten what it was.

"I can see you're going to be great company!"

The big man lay down again and went to sleep.

It wasn't hard work looking after him, fetching him food and water. Changing his bedding, when the guards allowed it. Leading him every day to the mill where he worked with the other slaves, taking his turn at pushing

the big mill wheel. It was work for donkeys, but it amused the Philistines to see it being done by men.

The worst times were the evening parties when Samson was sent for to entertain the guests. While the boy led him around, the Philistines teased and taunted him, pelted him with scraps of food and prodded him with knives and sticks. They gave him choice bits of food to eat, smothered with mustard.

They offered him wine and gave him vinegar instead.

"Don't worry, boy," whispered Samson. "It's me they're laughing at, not you."

But the boy could see that part of the joke was watching the big, blind man so helpless without a little dumb boy to lead him.

They treated the boy as if he really were a dog, patting him on the head and offering him little tidbits to eat under the table. One evening someone gave him a piece of honeycomb, which he took back to the prison cell. He broke it in two and gave half to Samson.

"Out of the strong came forth sweetness," murmured Samson. "That's a riddle. Do you know what it means? Of course you don't."

He chewed on the honeycomb for a bit, then licked his fingers and wiped them on his tunic. "Once, I was courting this girl. A Philistine girl, as it happens. I haven't always fought the Philistines. They were here, running our country. Let's try and be friends, I thought.

"Anyway, I was on my way to visit her one day, walking along a lonely country road, when a lion stepped out of the bushes, straight in front of me.

"It stopped and looked at me, surprised as I was. Then it gave a snarl and a roar and leaped straight for my throat."

Samson paused for effect.

The boy had stopped eating, his brown eyes wide with fear and wonder.

"I know what you're thinking," said Samson. "You're wondering how it is that I'm still here to tell the tale. Well, I killed it, didn't I? Broke it's neck with my bare hands and left it

lying by the road.

"It wasn't a very big lion," he added. "Not worth telling anybody about. So I didn't.

"A few weeks later, I was on my way to my wedding, past the very same spot. There was the lion's carcass, still lying there, a bit the worse for wear by now, and right inside it a swarm of bees had built a nest.

"While I was helping myself to some of the honeycomb, I thought of this riddle to ask at the wedding. You know what weddings are like." He paused. "Well, perhaps you don't. Everyone has to be ready to sing a song or tell a story or a joke. So I make up this riddle to ask."

Samson cleared his throat and recited:

"Out of the eater came something to eat.
Out of the strong came something sweet.
What am I?

"My bride's brother said, 'And what's the penalty? What do we have to do if we can't guess the answer?' I hadn't thought about that. The only thing I could think of was that they might pay for my wedding clothes.

" 'And if we do guess it, then you have to give us a new suit of clothes?'

" 'That's right,' I said. I didn't realize at first that if I lost, I'd promised to give him and each of his friends a new suit of clothes. All thirty of them. All they had to do was give me one, between them. That's Philistines for you. Never trust a Philistine, even if he is your wife's brother.

"I should eat up that honey, if I were you, before it all drips on the floor. You haven't moved a muscle in minutes."

The boy made haste to eat up.

"Where was I? Oh yes. For three days they couldn't find the answer. Then do you know who tipped them off? My lovely new wife. She nagged and she cried and she kept saying husbands and wives shouldn't have secrets from one another. In the end I told her, just so I could get some sleep.

"Next day, when I came into the dining room her brother had all his friends lined up to meet me.

"'All together now!' he said. 'One. Two. Three?'

"And all together they chorused:

'What is sweeter than honey?
What is stronger than a lion?'

"The very words I'd made up for the answer! How they laughed at the dumb Israelite! How was he going to pay for thirty new suits of clothes?"

Samson leaned back against the wall and said softly, "They got their new clothes. That night I went out and killed thirty Philistines, took their clothes and handed them over in the morning, still covered in blood.

"Of course, the wedding was off after that. The bride's father married her off to another man."

The boy was wondering if any girl would marry this great scarecrow as he was now. He fetched some water to wash the big man's face and hair. Tomorrow he would find something to use as a comb.

The boy became an expert beggar.

He couldn't speak, but he would fix someone with his eyes, unblinkingly, until they either kicked him away, or gave him some of what they were eating. A little of it the boy ate himself; the rest he took back to Samson.

In return the big man told him stories, always about himself and his great strength. He didn't seem to know any others. After that incident at the wedding, he'd set out to wage a one-man war against the Philistines.

Time after time he had burned their crops.

Times without number he had sprung an ambush, until they were afraid to travel the roads even in broad daylight, without an escort of soldiers.

He told the boy of the time the Philistines had him trapped inside the city, with the gates locked against him, only to find next morning that Samson had carried off the gates, gateposts and all, during the night and dumped them on top of the next hill when he got tired of carrying them.

At last his own people, the Israelites, had been frightened into handing him over, tied hand and foot, for the Philistines to collect. At which point he'd burst out of the ropes, grabbed the jawbone of an ass, which happened to be handy, and killed a thousand Philistines before making his escape.

"Was it really a thousand?" Samson frowned.

"They say it was. I was too busy to count exactly. It must have been quite a few, or they wouldn't have put such a price on my head.

"Then I fell in love with this girl, Delilah.

"The Philistines soon found out about it. They've got spies everywhere. First they threatened her and then they offered her the reward. Poor Delilah! I don't blame her. It was a lot of money.

"I told her about the vow my mother had made before I was born. God promised her that He'd make me strong if she vowed my hair would never be cut. It's a terrible thing to break a vow like that. Even if you didn't make it. Even if it's not your fault it was broken.

"I went to sleep with the strength of ten men. When I woke up, it was like one of those nightmares where you can't move a muscle, however hard you try. I was trussed up like a chicken ready for the pot, with no more strength than a chicken to get free.

"Delilah had cut off my hair while I slept. She tied me up, then called the Philistines.

"There they all were, standing around

laughing at me struggling to get free.

"But I could still see the fear deep inside them. They blinded me and they starved me half to death and I can still smell the fear on them every time they come near."

The big man was silent for a while. Then he said: "Do you think it will ever grow back?"

For an answer, the boy took Samson's hand and guided it so he could feel the hair hanging thick and straight, almost to his shoulders.

"That's good," murmured Samson. "That's very good. I thought I was feeling stronger."

You would never have known it, watching him working at the mill, pushing the great wheel around, taking his turn with the other slaves. He still seemed no stronger than the rest.

But the boy could tell.

The boy tended him carefully. The cooks in the kitchen got used to seeing him there, foraging for scraps from the banqueting hall. They pressed great bundles of leftovers into his hands, murmuring to each other as he scurried away:

"I don't know where he puts it all."

"He must have hollow legs."

Nobody seemed to notice that Samson was putting on weight. As soon as they found that he was not giving any trouble, the guards hardly looked at him at all. Nobody cared whether his hair was growing or not. The story had been told so many times that it all seemed a bit silly now, the idea that a man could be so much stronger than the rest, all because of his long hair.

But it would soon be a year to the day since Samson had been captured. The Philistines were planning to celebrate in a big way. They'd built a special banqueting hall—and only just got it finished in time. Samson had to be there, of course.

The guard thrust an extra pitcher of water into the cell.

"Smarten him up a bit," he told the boy. "We can't have the guest of honor smelling like a dunghill."

"Yes, smarten me up," said Samson softly.

"Tie my hair in seven braids, the way I used to wear it."

He caused quite a stir when the boy led him into the hall.

There were no jokes. No horseplay.

They just stared, openmouthed.

This was the man who had killed thirty men in a night, just to settle a debt.

This was the man who broke down the city gates and carried them away.

This was the man who fought off a small army, with only the jawbone of an ass in his hand.

This was Samson!

If only Samson had had his eyes, the hall would have been empty in two minutes flat. But what could he do without his eyes?

Some of them got up and walked slowly around him, as if he were an ancient monument, then went back to their places, thinking this was something to tell their grandchildren— I was this close to him! As close as I am now to you. After that, they lost interest.

"Show me around," whispered Samson. "I want to know all about this place."

For half an hour or more, the boy led him around. Samson ran his hands over the stone blocks that formed the walls.

"Typical Philistine work!" he said scornfully.

"A child could do better. Stones just piled up all anyhow! See where I can almost get my hand between them? Now let's have a look at the pillars . . ."

He measured the size of them, paced out the distance between, kicked at the base of them.

"Just as I thought! No proper foundations."

All the time, the boy sensed that he was putting a picture together in his mind's eye.

"Sounds like another party going on, up on the roof," he remarked. "That's not safe. Could bring the whole place down—with a bit of help, eh?" The boy saw that he was smiling.

"Those two pillars over there, I think. Lead me to them!"

When they got there, he rested his hand against the first pillar for a moment, as if he was suddenly very tired.

"Lord, make me strong again," he whispered, "one last time." Then, with a quick jerk, he snapped the iron chain between his wrists and stretched out his hand, feeling for the other pillar.

"Time for you to go, boy," said Samson. "I'm giving us both our freedom. Freedom, that's the word. So don't cry for me, do you hear? Go, I said. Run! Run for your life!"

Samson braced himself between the pillars. Slowly he began to push them apart.

The boy ran.

Behind him he heard the shouts of alarm as people realized too late what the big man was doing. A crash and screams as the roof timbers began to tumble, bringing the people on top down among the party guests.

On and on he ran, while in the hall people jammed the doorways, fell, or trampled one another underfoot.

One by one the pillars fell and the walls began to crumble. Some of the trapped men tried to force a way through and only brought down more stones.

They say three thousand died that night, but the boy only cared for one. When daylight came, he was still sitting on a hill overlooking the city, watching for some sign of life from the mass of dust and rubble.

But there was none. Only a few would-be rescuers standing around, wondering where to

begin and knowing it wouldn't be worth the trouble.

He wasn't going to cry. Samson had told him not to.

When they killed his family, burned his village and took him away to be a slave, he never shed a tear, nor spoke a word. All the tears and words were locked away in a place so deep inside him, he wasn't sure he could ever find it again.

Then a small tear found its own way out and rolled down his cheek. Angrily he brushed it away.

A small voice whispered: "Freedom."

He looked around to see who had spoken and found no one there. It must have been his own voice he had heard.

He tried it again: "Freedom." It sounded good. Soon other words might follow it, but this one would do for now.

The boy stood up and turned his back on the Philistine town. He spread out his arms like a bird in flight and ran, swooping and leaping, down into the valley.

"Freedom!" he shouted.

And from every side, the hills answered: "Freedom!"

THE GOOD DAUGHTER

Two women on the road, walking westward.

Walking, walking. Two women: one old, one young. Stopping to beg for a bite to eat.

"I'll work for it," the young one said. "I'll work for both of us. My mother is too old."

"Your mother?"

"Yes, Naomi is my mother. I am Ruth."

The old woman nodded fondly: "My daughter. The only family I have left."

"We're going home," said Ruth.

Mother and daughter? How could that be? The young one was clearly a Moabite, the old one a Jew. How could they both be going home?

Most of the time they walked in silence. Naomi had a lot to think about. Ten years ago, when she last walked along this road, going eastward, toward Moab, she'd had a husband and two fine sons.

That was the year of the famine. Not a drop of water. Not a blade of grass. They'd eaten all the food they had stored. Spent all their money. Still the prices kept rising and the rains didn't come. They sold Naomi's jewelry, family ornaments, spare pots and pans, all but the clothes they stood up in. They ate the seed corn. If the rains came now, there would be nothing to plant. So they locked up the house and joined the stream of refugees on the road going east to Moab.

The Moabites were good people. They welcomed the refugees into their homes and gave them whatever they had to spare. The men found work. Naomi's sons both married local girls, Orpah and Ruth. It seemed sensible to stay in Moab. For ten years they lived there.

Then suddenly Naomi's world seemed to fall apart. Her husband and both her sons died, all in the space of a few weeks.

The three women, Naomi, Ruth, and Orpah, mourned together. At last Naomi said to the two girls: "You must leave me now. Go back to your parents' homes."

"We can't leave you alone," said Ruth. "I will look after you, as a daughter should."

She helped Orpah pack her things and hugged her and kissed her when the time came to say good-bye.

"Be happy," whispered Ruth.

"And you," said Orpah.

"We will be," Ruth promised, and turning to Naomi, she said: "Your people will be my people. Your God will be my God. I've decided what we're going to do. We're going home."

So here they were, walking westward along the road which Naomi had never forgotten. If she closed her eyes now, she could still see it as it was during the famine. She could smell the stink of it: dirt and disease, death and decay.

Then she would open them again and see green pastures, fields of barley turning golden in the sun and plump fruit ripening in the orchards.

Naomi's step grew lighter. Now and then she smiled, imagining how her old home would look, with the little plot of land beside it. The

121

neat rows of vegetables. There would be plenty of room to grow all the food they needed and enough land left over to keep a goat and a few chickens. Silent all the way from Moab, Naomi couldn't stop chattering now about her memories and her plans for the house and that little piece of land.

She'd forgotten one thing. It was ten long years since anyone plowed or weeded that land. Ten years since they last closed the door. Now it was only the mass of weeds that kept the door from falling off its hinges. Inside—when they finally managed to get inside—part of the roof had crumbled, leaving an easy way in and out for birds nesting among the rafters. There were bones of dead animals littering the floor and the whole place stank of foxes.

"Never mind," said Ruth. "We've slept in places not much better along the way—and had to pay for it. You go down to the well and fetch some water. I'll start clearing up."

Down the village street went Naomi to the well.

After her the whisper ran: "Isn't that Naomi?"

"Naomi?"

"Naomi who went to Moab. In the year of the famine."

"That was ten years ago. Is she really back?"

Women stopped what they were doing and reached for their water jugs. There was nothing that couldn't wait until after they'd fetched more water from the well.

"Naomi!"

"Welcome back!"

"How's your husband?"

"Where are the boys?"

"I heard they were married."

It was all too much for poor Naomi. "Don't call me Naomi," she said sadly. "I've lost everything—my husband, my sons. And look at my poor little house. Call me Mara from now on. Mara means bitterness. My life is all bitterness now."

Then she heard Ruth's soft voice: "To me you will always be Naomi. Naomi means the pleasant one, doesn't it? And so you are. I came after you to help you carry the water. I should never have sent you on your own."

Naomi started to cry again: "How can I say my life is all bitterness, when I have a daughter. This is Ruth. My daughter."

"And so many friends, too," said Ruth.

All through the evening there was a stream of visitors to the tumbledown house, bringing little welcome-back presents: a loaf of bread, goat cheese, a dish of olives, even a straw mattress to sleep on—"No, no! Keep it. I really don't know why I've hung on to it since my son left home."

Only the poor really understand what it's like to have nothing at all.

"All the same," said Naomi, "we can't live on charity."

"Of course not," said Ruth. "Tomorrow I'll go and see what I can glean from the harvest fields."

In the days before harvesting was done by machinery, poor people had the right to follow the harvesters, collecting up any odd stalks of barley that they dropped.

It was hard work, gleaning out in the broiling sun all day, picking up the stalks one at a time. Think how many times you would have to bend down and stand up again before you'd collected a full sheaf of barley! The regular gleaners were tough, boisterous girls who'd done it all their lives. Naturally the farmer, Boaz, couldn't help noticing the quiet stranger.

"Who is she?" he asked.

He must have been the only person around who didn't already know the story of Naomi and her daughter.

"Naomi?" said Boaz. "I had a cousin who married a woman called Naomi. But they went away during the famine ten years ago."

"That'll be the one."

"Tell the other workers to treat her gently," said Boaz. "If the men ahead of her drop a few more stalks than usual, turn a blind eye."

Naomi exclaimed in surprise at the amount of barley Ruth brought home that evening: "You've done this before!"

"No." Ruth shook her head. "The men ahead of me were careless. I think Boaz told them to be. I suppose it's his way of being kind to his poor relations."

"Boaz?"

"I think he's a cousin of your husband's."

"He's quite old, then?"

"Oh, no! He can still do a full day's work

with the rest of them." Then Ruth blushed, because she shouldn't have noticed what Boaz was doing.

She had to speak to him, of course, when he spoke to her. If he told her she could eat with his servants in the middle of the day and gave her extra food to take home to Naomi, it would have been rude as well as silly to refuse.

Naomi was getting to be more like her own self again. Instead of two sons, she now had a daughter and like any good mother, she was determined to do the best she could for her.

One day she said to Ruth: "About the piece of land out back. We'll never get it straight, you know. I think I might sell it. Under our law it should be offered first to my husband's nearest relative. I think that's Boaz. Perhaps you could mention it to him next time you see him."

Ruth was surprised to see how worried Boaz looked when she told him. It was such a little piece of land, compared to what he had already.

"I'm not the nearest relative," he said. "Tell Naomi there is another man who has a better claim."

Naomi, when she heard this, was still bent on selling.

"Ask Boaz to arrange it," she said. "This is men's business."

So Boaz went to the man, and the man listened to what Boaz had to say. He thought about it. Then he said, "I'll buy."

Boaz's heart sank right down to his sandals. "Then by our law," he said, "you know you must take the widow, too. Will you still buy?"

The man seemed to think very long and hard about it. All the while he was watching Boaz's face. At last he grinned and shook his head: "In that case, I won't buy. I've got more than enough women in my house already, including wife and a mother-in-law."

Boaz was free to buy the land, but he knew now it wasn't really the land he wanted.

"Naomi," he said, "May I have your daughter to be my wife?"

"You'd better ask her," said Naomi. "It's nothing to do with me."

Boaz threw back his head and laughed: "Oh, Naomi!" he cried. "Nothing to do with you? It's everything to do with you! What put it into your head to sell that piece of land, if it wasn't finding a husband for your daughter? You've missed your trade. You should have been a matchmaker. But Ruth, dear Ruth, will you marry me?"

It was seeing Boaz laugh at the way Naomi had arranged it all that made Ruth's mind up for her. Of course she said yes. There'd be no point in telling the story otherwise.

The wedding party lasted a whole week.

Naomi thought she could never be happier, until a year later, when they presented her with a grandchild. In time that grandchild would grow up to be grandfather to a line of kings. Of course Naomi didn't know that. It was enough for her that at last she'd got a grandchild to spoil.

"Of course he's my grandchild," said Naomi proudly, as she paraded him round the village. "Ruth's my daughter, isn't she? Well, isn't she? The best daughter a mother ever had!"

GIANT-KILLER!

The Lord is my shepherd.
I have everything I need.

No: too clumsy.

David thought for a moment then began again:

The Lord is my shepherd
De-dum-de-dum-de-dum (Leave that bit out for the moment).

He makes me lie down in green pastures.
He leads me beside still waters.

That was good. He must remember that bit.

Except that, as usual, the sheep were leading him. They knew their own way to the next grazing ground. All he had to do was watch for strays wandering off or wild animals on the lookout for an easy meal. It left him plenty of time to think and make up poems. Sometimes

he made up music, too, and turned the poems into songs.

His brothers had gone off to fight for the king against the Philistines, leaving David behind to mind the sheep. David liked looking after the sheep, so that was all right.

The Lord is my shepherd.

I shall lack nothing.

Better.

"David!" a voice called from the other side of the valley. His father's voice.

There he was, hurrying toward him.

"David, you must come home at once."

"Why?" asked David. "What about the sheep?"

"They can graze in the home pasture until you come back. I want you to take a supply of food to your brothers."

"Where are they now?"

"The army's still at Elah. They haven't moved in over a month and they're running out of everything."

First thing next morning, David was on his way with the supplies for his soldier-brothers. As he neared the camp, he could hear shouting, the sound of trumpets and the clash of swords. The battle must have started! David quickened his step.

But when he came closer, he saw that everything was quiet in the king's camp—and on the far side of the valley, where the Philistines had pitched their tents.

"I thought I heard fighting," said David, as he handed over the food. "Voices. Trumpets."

"Oh, that!" said Eliab, his eldest brother. "You get used to that."

"It happens every hour, on the hour, all day long," said Abinadab.

"It's boring," yawned Shammah.

"Come on," said Eliab. "I'll show you."

He led him through the camp toward the stream at the valley bottom.

From the Philistine camp came a blast of trumpets. Armed men came marching out, but not to fight, just to show off the size of the one who came after them. He was a giant, taller than two men one on top of the other and broad to match. The metal in his armor would have made three medium-sized war chariots.

"Goliath!" whispered Eliab.

Goliath strode out in front of the Philistine soldiers and bellowed so that both camps could hear: "King Saul! King Saul! Come out and fight! Or send your champion to fight me, man to man! Winner takes all!"

Then the Philistines rattled their swords against their shields, the trumpets blared, and Goliath roared and the Philistines jeered. The men of the King's army turned away and pretended not to hear.

"Does he mean what he says?" asked David, as they walked back to the others. "Winner takes all? The war will be over?"

"He means it," said Eliab.

"Then why doesn't someone take him on?"

"And lose the war for us? Are you mad?"

"Our man might win."

"Oh, yes?"

"Goliath's just a man. He can be killed. I think I can even see a way it might be done."

"Don't be stupid. You stick to what you know about—minding sheep."

David was going to say that that was where he got the idea, but he thought he'd better not.

Eliab told the others what David had said. They laughed at him and passed the joke on . . .

This shepherd was offering to take on Goliath . . .

Next day, David was summoned to the king's tent.

He was met there by a wide-eyed boy not much older than himself.

"I'm Jonathan, the king's son. I'm in charge while he's sick."

"Saul's got a headache," one of the soldiers muttered.

"Had it for weeks."

"Name of Goliath."

Jonathan glared at them. Behind him some-one said: "Girls get headaches. Kings fight battles."

"You see how it is," said Jonathan to David. "They told me they'd found us a champion. Now I can see it was just another joke."

"I'll be your champion," said David.

"You?" Jonathan stared at him. Looking at him, as one boy to another, Jonathan could see that David had a plan. A good one. But he wasn't going to tell anyone what it was.

Jonathan made up his mind. He ducked inside the darkened tent where his father lay.

"Go away," moaned Saul. "I'm not well. I can't see anyone."

"We've found a champion to fight Goliath."

"Send him out to fight, then. Don't bother me," was all the answer he got.

"The trouble is, he's got no proper armor or anything," said Jonathan.

"Lend him mine, then. I'm not using it, am I? Ooh, my poor head! I think I'm going to die. I wish I could die."

So they fetched the king's armor and put it on David. A padded leather tunic that came down below his knees, with hundreds of metal plates stitched on, like fish scales. A helmet of solid bronze that rested on his shoulders. A great two-handed sword, which trailed along the floor when they buckled it around David's waist.

"Off you go, then" said Jonathan. "Good luck!"

David didn't budge.

"Changed your mind?" said Jonathan. "I don't blame you."

"It's not that," said David. "I just can't move in all this armor. Please tell them to take it off. It was kind of the king to lend it to me, but really I don't need it."

So David walked out to meet Goliath dressed in his tunic and sandals, his shepherd's sling held loosely in his hand. It was just a small piece of leather with two strings, but it could fling a pebble with deadly force. He had killed a lion with it. And a bear. And driven off more wild beasts than he could count.

He'd never aimed it at a man before. He wasn't even sure that he could do it.

The Lord is my shepherd.

I shall not want.

He makes me lie down in green pastures.

He leads me beside the still waters.

That was it! Oh, if he should die now without ever having the chance to put the words to music!

He stopped at the stream and bent down, looking for pebbles of just the right size and shape, weighing them in his hand.

He'd picked out five, when he felt a great shadow fall across him.

It was not the giant, just a shadow passing across the sun.

Even though I walk through the valley of the shadow of death,

I fear no evil,

Because you are with me . . .

David stood up and moved forward again.

From the Philistine camp came the sound of trumpets and the rumble of marching feet. Men, marching toward him.

Stand still. Take a deep breath.

Out strode Goliath, as he'd done so many times before.

This time someone stood waiting for him. A boy in tunic and sandals, quietly tying a leather

string around the middle finger of his right hand.

"Get back!" roared Goliath. "I don't make war on children."

"Get back yourself," said David. "Or I shall have to kill you."

The giant was puzzled. He wasn't used to people standing up to him. Usually they ran away.

"Go back," said David. "Or I will kill you."

He saw fear in Goliath's eyes. But the giant couldn't turn back: the Philistines would never let him.

Slowly he raised his javelin. The boy was so small! At this range, the javelin would take his head clean off.

David knew that, too. Five pebbles was four too many. One chance was all he'd get.

He fitted a pebble into the sling, raised it above his head, and whirled it around, faster and faster, judging his aim, his distance.

Goliath drew back his arm.

It was now or never!

The pebble flew so fast, it was invisible.

He thought he'd missed.

The giant stood still, with the javelin poised, ready to throw.

He looked no different—except for a small, dark hole in the middle of his forehead.

A look of complete surprise spread over his face. And then he fell, like a mighty tree toppled by the woodman's ax.

Suddenly the Israelites were cheering, moving forward, as the Philistines grabbed whatever they could carry and headed for the hills.

David let the tide of men sweep past him, then he made his way back to the king's tent.

"Go in," said Jonathan. "Go in and tell him yourself that the giant's dead!"

David plucked at his dusty tunic and pointed to his worn sandals: "I can't go in like this,"

"Of course you can't," said Jonathan. "I'll lend you some of my things."

Quickly David put them on. Robe. Boots. Belt and sword.

Jonathan grinned: "You look almost like a king yourself. Just a minute." He went inside the tent.

"Good news, Father. Your champion's here."

The only answer was a groan. Saul's head hurt worse than ever. It muddled his thinking. Hadn't they had this conversation earlier in the day?

"You can go in now," said Jonathan to David. "Just remember not to speak until you're spoken to."

David stood by the king's bed for a long time,

waiting to be spoken to. It gave him time to look around.

Quite early on in the king's illness, one of the doctors had suggested that soft music might do the king some good. Perhaps it was the wrong sort of music, but two minutes after they sent him into the tent, the musician came running out again with the king's spear close behind. He'd probably run clean out of the country by the time they found out he'd left his harp behind. There it still lay, waiting, it seemed, for David.

He picked it up and plucked at the strings. He'd thought of a tune to go with his poem, and he was itching to try it out before he forgot it.

"Well, play if you're going to!" snarled a voice from the bed.

David began to play his new song.

The king said nothing more, so David went on playing till he was sure the king was sound asleep.

The Lord is my shepherd, I shall not want;
He makes me lie down in green pastures.
He leads me beside still waters;
He restores my soul.
He leads me in paths of righteousness for His
    name's sake.

Even though I walk through the valley of the
    shadow of death,
I fear no evil;
for Thou art with me;
Thy rod and Thy staff, they comfort me.

Thou preparest a table before me
in the presence of my enemies;
Thou anointest my head with oil,
my cup overflows.

Surely goodness and mercy shall follow me
    all the days of my life;
and I shall dwell in the house of the Lord
    forever.

SOLOMON THE WISE

What is it that makes a good king? Is it winning battles against his country's enemies? Is it being rich and powerful? Collecting taxes, building great palaces? If not, what is it?

The trouble with being made king is that no one can teach you how to do it. They put a crown on your head and show you to the cheering crowds, and then it's all up to you.

That's how it was with Solomon. And he was very young to be a king.

How can I be a good king? He worried about it every day and at night the question ran through his dreams.

In his dreams one night he heard God say: "I can make you a great king, Solomon, but you must choose. Will you be Solomon the

Conqueror? Solomon the Magnificent? Or Solomon the Wise?" Solomon thought carefully. "Let me be wise," he said at last. "The rest doesn't matter, if I can only rule my people wisely." "A good choice," said God. "A wise choice. Solomon the Wise it shall be."

He never became Solomon the Conqueror, because he was always wise enough to see a way of making peace with his enemies and still be strong.

A kingdom at peace, which doesn't waste its money and young men on wars, soon becomes rich. Solomon the Wise became Solomon the Magnificent, whether he wanted it or not. He built a temple for God who gave him wisdom, and that temple was the wonder of the world.

Yet Solomon the Wise still held court every day, when the poorest of his subjects could come and ask for justice. One day—the end of a long, long day of trials and arguments, questions and answers, and judgments given—two women stood before him: two women with one baby, both claiming to be his mother.

They were two poor women who shared a house, each with a baby much the same age. Each took a turn to watch both babies while the other one went out to work. Then one of the babies died and both women claimed the baby that was left as her own.

One said: "How can she know which baby it was that died? She wasn't there."

The other admitted: "I was out at work. But I'd know my own child among a thousand!"

It was no good leaving the baby to decide. He smiled at one and laughed with the other when she tickled his toes; seized the finger of one when she offered it and grabbed for the necklace the other wore. He didn't really care which was his mother.

But the women cared:

"He's mine!"

"You can see he's mine!"

"Give him to me!"

"Come to Mommy!"

Solomon pretended to yawn. "Just do what we always do in these cases," he told his courtiers.

The courtiers were puzzled: "Do what we always do?"

"Give them half each. Send for the executioner."

The executioner came, with his long, curved sword.

Solomon pointed to the baby: "Cut it in half."

The executioner raised his sword and took careful aim. Solomon was Solomon the Wise, so he must know what he was doing.

Then one of the women threw herself between the baby and the shining sword.

"Don't kill my baby!" she cried. Gently she gathered him up and offered him to the other woman. "Give him to her, if you will, but let him live."

Triumphantly the other woman went to take the baby, but Solomon stopped her. To the woman who held the baby he said: "Keep your baby. You spoke like his true mother."

Hugging her baby tight, the woman fell on her knees: "They are right to call you Solomon the Wise. May your name live forever!"

The other woman knelt too. What happened to someone who lied to the king?

Solomon spoke to her gently: "It doesn't matter that you lied to me. Stop lying to yourself. Stop lying to your poor, dead baby. Admit he is dead. Go home and weep for him and let him rest in peace. Be friends."

He took her hand and gave it to the mother of the baby, and the two women went home together.

DANIEL AND
THE LIONS

King Darius of Persia was in a fix and he didn't see how he could get out of it. He'd have to have his best friend thrown to the lions. Not just his best friend. Daniel was his best adviser, too—better than all his other advisers put together. Daniel was honest. Daniel was a prophet. Daniel could tell you the meaning of your dreams.

On top of that, Daniel was a foreigner, a Jew, who said all the Persian gods were false gods. There was only one God, said Daniel. Faithfully he prayed to God, three times a day.

Put all those things together and you couldn't expect Daniel to be popular with the king's other advisers. They plotted to get rid of Daniel once and for all. They persuaded the king to pass a law so that anyone who asked a favor from anyone—man or god—except from the king, would be thrown into the lions' den.

It seemed like a good idea. The ministers explained that it would stop people offering bribes to judges to get a verdict in their favor, or asking people at court to find nice, well-paid jobs for their sons and nephews.

Darius did wonder at the time why it said man or god. People didn't ask the Persian gods for favors. The Persian gods didn't care about what happened to anyone, so long as the sacrifices kept coming.

If he'd wondered a bit more, he might have remembered that Daniel's God was different. Daniel's God seemed to be someone you could talk to. Daniel's God cared.

Daniel realized right away that the law was aimed at just one person—him. But that didn't stop him praying to God just as he'd always done. It was just what the ministers had been hoping for.

"He's praying to his God again."

"Asking for favors!"

"He knows it's against the law now, but he's still doing it!"

"Now you're going to throw him to the lions, aren't you?"

"It's all right," said Daniel. "I understand. If the king doesn't obey his own laws, who will?"

"It was a stupid law," said Darius. "I don't know why I passed it."

"Never mind," said Daniel. "When I come out again, we'll talk about changing it."

The king clutched at a little straw of hope drifting by on the wind: "When you come out?" he said.

"The law only says you've got to throw me in the lions' den," said Daniel. "It doesn't say they've got to eat me."

"That's true," said Darius.

"See you in the morning, then," said Daniel, as the door closed behind him. "God willing."

The king stood outside, listening for the lions' roar, telling him that Daniel was being torn into little pieces.

Nothing. Perhaps it was all over already. Sadly the king walked away.

He could see now what a fool he'd been, but that was no help to Daniel. No one could help Daniel now, unless . . .

He might try praying to the sort of god who cared. Darius got down on his knees and began:

"God of Daniel. You don't know me—well, perhaps you do. Daniel says you know everything. So you know already that he's in trouble and he really needs your help . . ."

Meanwhile, in the lions' den, everything was quiet.

The lions were lying in a corner. They looked up when Daniel came in. What, dinner time already? No, it couldn't be. Dinner always ran about making a lot of noise.

The lions lay down again and Daniel stood watching them until one by one the lions fell

asleep, dreaming of sunbaked plains and pools of sweet water near a secret cave. Wild deer scattering . . . the chase . . . the kill . . . Then dozing in the shade, watching the young ones playing.

King Darius had a terrible night. He gave up praying and tried to sleep, but couldn't. So he got up and walked around. Lay down again, still couldn't sleep. Sent for his musicians. Sent them away again. Got up and walked around some more. In the end he sat curled up by the window, wishing it were morning.

As soon as the sun's rim peeked over the horizon, he was off downstairs to the lions' den.

Should he knock?

Darius decided against it. There was no way anyone could open the door from the inside.

"Daniel?" he called softly. "Are you still there?"

Daniel chuckled. "Where would I go, Darius? Yes, I'm still here."

"What about the lions?"

"They're still here, too. Asleep at the moment. Can I come out now, please?"

As the door opened and Daniel slipped quietly out, the king looked past him at the slumbering lions.

"Looks like they weren't hungry," said Daniel.

"It was a miracle," said Darius. "It was your God. I put in a word for you last night. Asked your God to protect you."

"So He did," said Daniel, "by making sure the lions just weren't hungry."

Then King Darius sent out a decree to all the nations of the Empire, saying that they should honor Daniel's God, who saved his servant Daniel from the lions.

THE RELUCTANT PROPHET

"I'm not going to Nineveh," said Jonah. "And that's that!"

"You must, Jonah," said God.

"Why?"

"Because I say so. Nineveh is a wicked city and I'm going to destroy it in forty days' time. That's the message. I want you to deliver it."

"You're going to destroy a whole city? A hundred and twenty thousand people? Little babies, dogs, and all?" Jonah shook his head. "You won't do it."

"I will," said God.

"You'll change your mind. How will I look then, after prophesying the end of the city for forty days, when nothing happens? Why can't I do some nice prophecies for a change? The birth of a prince? A large harvest? I'm tired of

153

being Jonah Doom-and-gloom. Sometimes they throw things, you know."

He got up and dusted himself off. "I'm not going to Nineveh," he said firmly. "And you can't make me!"

He set off down the road toward the harbor.

"Where are you going?" asked God.

"Anywhere," replied Jonah. "So long as it's not Nineveh."

He spoke to the captain of the first boat he came to: "Where are you bound for?" he asked.

"Tarshish," said the captain.

"That sounds far enough away. I'll take a one-way ticket."

"Deck or hold?"

"Hold," said Jonah. "I'd like to get some sleep."

The ship sailed out of harbor on a calm sea with a following wind and not a cloud in the sky.

But as soon as they were out of sight of land, things quickly began to change. Black clouds piled up on the horizon and spilled over, tumbling toward the little ship, with a rumbling of thunder you could feel through the soles of your feet. Lightning danced up and down the rigging. The rain began to fall as if

someone were pouring it out of a bucket. The wind blew from all directions at once, whipping up the waves, ten, twenty, thirty feet high.

Jonah slept through it all, until the captain came to find him. All the other passengers were up on deck, praying to their different gods. Would Jonah come and join in, please?

Surely some god would hear their prayers.

Jonah's style of praying was a bit different from the rest.

"It's you, isn't it?" he yelled. "Don't pretend it's not. I know it's you. Just because I wouldn't go to Nineveh!"

He listened carefully to the next roll of thunder, then he turned to the captain. "If you want to save your ship," he said, "you'd better throw me overboard."

"I can't do that!" said the captain.

But the other passengers had heard what Jonah said.

To save a lot of argument, he jumped.

Soon the ship was just a dot on the far horizon.

The sea grew calm and the sun came out. It was really quite a nice day for a swim. Another ship would come along soon and rescue him. Or else he'd find a desert island, build himself a little cabin, and live on fish and fruit.

Then everything went black. A huge fish had swallowed him whole.

It was warm and dry inside, but very dark. There was nothing for Jonah to do but some good, hard thinking.

After three days and nights, the creature coughed him up onto a sandy beach.

Jonah picked himself up. "All right," he said. "I'll go to Nineveh!"

He hitched up his robe and set off, still in a very bad temper. There's nothing like a bit of genuine bad temper to add spice to a prophecy of doom and gloom.

Nineveh was a place to make anybody angry. Beggars sleeping in the streets—and dying there too. Nobody cared. Certainly not the rich folk, driving by in their chariots. All they cared about was getting richer. Poor men, jealous of the rich, stole from their neighbors. It was not enough to make them rich, but if they used it to gamble with, they might get lucky. Fights broke out over the gambling tables. Some men were wounded. Some of them died. Small children crept out of the shadows to steal the dead men's shoes to sell. What else could they do? Their mothers had no money to feed them. A terrible place.

Grab what you can and spend, spend, spend, because tomorrow may never come. That was Nineveh.

Now here was this wild-eyed, angry little man, smelling strongly of fish, telling them there were only forty tomorrows left—thirty-nine—thirty-eight . . .

"And serves you right!" yelled Jonah.

Then he retired to a safe distance, out of range of any earthquakes, thunderbolts or tidal waves that God might be getting ready.

The people of Nineveh went about quietly, thoughtfully. What was the point of being rich, if there was so little time left? Let's all be a bit kinder to one another, since we're all in the same boat. They prayed for a miracle. "We're sorry, God. We know sorry doesn't make it better, but we are truly sorry."

The fortieth day came and went.

And the forty-first.

Nineveh was still there.

Jonah sat sulking in the shade of a small tree on a hill overlooking the city.

"I've done my bit," he said. "Now you do yours. Go on! Destroy them!"

God said nothing.

In the morning the little tree was dead, the leaves at the tip of each branch all curled and yellow, the rest already fallen.

"Poor thing," said Jonah.

"You're sorry for the tree?" said God.

"Of course I am," said Jonah. "It wasn't much of a tree, but it was doing its best."

"So are the people of Nineveh now," said God. "Aren't I allowed to be sorry for them? I'm giving them another chance."

"I just wish you'd let me do a nice prophecy now and then," grumbled Jonah.

"If you smiled a bit, I might," said God.

"Like this?" said Jonah, baring his teeth.

"Oh, Jonah!"

He heard a strange sound all around him that might just have been the wind.

Or it might have been God laughing.